Selected S...
HONORÉ D...

Books in this Series:

Selected Stories by O. Henry

Selected Stories by Anton Chekhov

Selected Stories by Guy de Maupassant

Selected Stories by Mark Twain

Selected Stories by Edgar Allan Poe

Selected Stories by Rudyard Kipling

Selected Stories by Saki

Selected Stories by Oscar Wilde

Selected Stories by Honoré de Balzac

Selected Stories by Charles Dickens

Selected Stories by D.H. Lawrence

Selected Stories by H.G. Wells

Selected Stories by Jack London

Selected Stories by Joseph Conrad

Selected Stories by Leo Tolstoy

Selected Stories by Sir Arthur Conan Doyle

Selected Stories by
HONORÉ DE BALZAC

RUPA

Published by
Rupa Publications India Pvt. Ltd 2014
7/16, Ansari Road, Daryaganj
New Delhi 110002

Sales Centres:
Allahabad Bengaluru Chennai
Hyderabad Jaipur Kathmandu
Kolkata Mumbai

Selection and Introduction copyright © Terry O'Brien 2014

All rights reserved.
No part of this publication may be reproduced, transmitted, or stored in a retrieval system, in any form or by any means, electronic, mechanical, photocopying, recording or otherwise, without the prior permission of the publisher.

ISBN: 978-81-291-3146-1

First impression 2014

10 9 8 7 6 5 4 3 2 1

Printed at Shree Maitrey Printech Pvt. Ltd., Noida

This book is sold subject to the condition that it shall not, by way of trade or otherwise, be lent, resold, hired out, or otherwise circulated, without the publisher's prior consent, in any form of binding or cover other than that in which it is published.

CONTENTS

Introduction　　　　　　　　　　　　　　　　　　　　　*vii*

1. The High Constable's Wife　　　　　　　　　　　　1
2. The Brothers-in-Arms　　　　　　　　　　　　　　18
3. Despair in Love　　　　　　　　　　　　　　　　　34
4. A Passion in the Desert　　　　　　　　　　　　　43
5. The Message　　　　　　　　　　　　　　　　　　59
6. The Red Inn　　　　　　　　　　　　　　　　　　74
7. The Purse　　　　　　　　　　　　　　　　　　　114
8. A Man of Business　　　　　　　　　　　　　　　148

INTRODUCTION

Honoré de Balzac (20 May 1799–18 August 1850) was a French novelist and playwright. His magnum opus was a sequence of short stories and novels collectively entitled *La Comédie humaine*, which presents a panorama of French life in the years after the 1815 fall of Napoleon Bonaparte.

Balzac is regarded as one of the founders of realism in European literature. He is renowned for his multifaceted characters. Many of Balzac's works have been made into or have inspired films, and they are a continuing source of inspiration for writers, film-makers and critics.

- A high constable of Armagnac is suspicious of who his wife's lover is—at which turn the lady employs all her wiles and charms to save her lover in the most ingenious fashion. What follows is tale of great passion and conflicting human emotions in 'The High Constable's Wife'.
- A tale of two brothers-in-arms, of their unbridled loyalty to each other and of a love that still comes second to that loyalty, 'The Brothers–in-Arms' is an example of exceptional storytelling.
- 'Despair in Love' is the story of love misunderstood, and of a lover so passionate and despairing of his beloved's love that he leaves the mark of his love on her by slashing her left cheek.
- 'A Passion in the Desert' is a beautiful allegorical tale of human

affection and the various stages of love, told through the event of one man getting stranded in the desert and befriending a jungle cat.
- 'The Message' is a story that begins with two men sharing a carriage and regaling each other with stories of the women they love. When the narrator's companion suddenly dies in a coach accident, the narrator is asked by the dying man to deliver the message of his death to his love.
- 'The Red Inn' begins with the daughter of a banker—who is the host of the party—asking a German gentleman, Hermann, to tell a frightening story. The story he proceeds to tell is chilling, but little do the guests know that the story has a direct bearing on one of the other guests at the party.
- 'The Purse' is a delicate portrayal of a friendship between two poor women and their neighbour, a young painter. Through this tale, Balzac shows not only a clear appreciation of the art world, but also depicts the treatment of the wives of fallen French soldiers—who are now poor widows.
- In 'A Man of Business', Balzac deals with the fine art of collecting debts as it was practised in Paris of the 1830s. The story begins with witty conversations about how debts are rarely paid by the wealthy, and goes on to relate such stories of debt.

Balzac influenced the writers of his time and beyond. He has been aptly called 'the French Dickens' and was a master in his own right.

1

THE HIGH CONSTABLE'S WIFE

The high constable of Armagnac espoused from the desire of a great fortune, the Countess Bonne, who was already considerably enamoured of little Savoisy, son of the chamberlain to his majesty King Charles the Sixth.

The constable was a rough warrior, miserable in appearance, tough in skin, thickly bearded, always uttering angry words, always busy hanging people, always in the sweat of battles, or thinking of other stratagems than those of love. Thus the good soldier, caring little to flavour the marriage stew, used his charming wife after the fashion of a man with more lofty ideas; of the which the ladies have a great horror, since they like not the joists of the bed to be the sole judges of their fondling and vigorous conduct.

Now the lovely Countess, as soon as she was grafted on the constable, only nibbled more eagerly at the love with which her heart was laden for the aforesaid Savoisy, which that gentleman clearly perceived.

Wishing both to study the same music, they would soon harmonize their fancies, and decipher the hieroglyphic; and this was a thing clearly demonstrated to the Queen Isabella, that Savoisy's horses were oftener stabled at the house of her cousin of Armagnac than in the Hotel St. Pol, where the chamberlain lived, since the destruction of his residence, ordered by the university, as everyone knows.

This discreet and wise princess, fearing in advance some unfortunate adventure for Bonne—the more so as the constable was as ready to brandish his broadsword as a priest to bestow benedictions—the said queen, as sharp as a dirk, said one day, while coming out from vespers, to her cousin, who was taking the holy water with Savoisy—

'My dear, don't you see some blood in that water?'

'Bah!' said Savoisy to the queen. 'Love likes blood, Madame.'

This the queen considered a good reply, and put it into writing, and later on, into action, when her lord the king wounded one of her lovers, whose business you see settled in this narrative.

You know by constant experience, that in the early time of love each of two lovers is always in great fear of exposing the mystery of the heart, and as much from the flower of prudence as from the amusement yielded by the sweet tricks of gallantry they play at who can best conceal their thoughts, but one day of forgetfulness suffices to inter the whole virtuous past. The poor woman is taken in her joy as in a lasso; her sweetheart proclaims his presence, or sometimes his departure, by some article of clothing—a scarf, a spur, left by some fatal chance, and there comes a stroke of the dagger that severs the web so gallantly woven by their golden delights. But when one is full of days, he should not make a wry face at death, and the sword of a husband is a pleasant death for a gallant, if there be pleasant deaths. So may be will finish the merry amours of the constable's wife.

One morning Monsieur d'Armagnac having lots of leisure time in consequence of the flight of the Duke of Burgundy, who was quitting Lagny, thought he would go and wish his lady good day, and attempted to wake her up in a pleasant enough fashion, so that she should not be angry; but she sunk in the heavy slumbers of the morning, replied to the action—

'Leave me alone, Charles!'

'Oh, oh,' said the constable, hearing the name of a saint who was not one of his patrons, 'I have a Charles on my head!'

Then, without touching his wife, he jumped out of the bed, and ran upstairs with his face flaming and his sword drawn, to the place where slept the countess's maid-servant, convinced that the said servant had a finger in the pie.

'Ah, ah, wench of hell!' cried he, to commence the discharge of his passion, 'say thy prayers, for I intend to kill thee instantly, because of the secret practices of Charles who comes here.'

'Ah, Monseigneur,' replied the woman, 'who told you that?'

'Stand steady, that I may rip thee at one blow if you do not confess to me every assignation given, and in what manner they have been arranged. If thy tongue gets entangled, if thou falterest, I will pierce thee with my dagger!'

'Pierce me through!' replied the girl, 'you will learn nothing.'

The constable, having taken this excellent reply amiss, ran her through on the spot, so mad was he with rage; and came back into his wife's chamber and said to his groom, whom, awakened by the shrieks of the girl, he met upon the stairs, 'Go upstairs; I've corrected Billette rather severely.'

Before he reappeared in the presence of Bonne he went to fetch his son, who was sleeping like a child, and led him roughly into her room. The mother opened her eyes pretty widely, you may imagine—at the cries of her little one; and was greatly terrified at seeing him in the hands of her husband, who had his right hand all bloody, and cast a fierce glance on the mother and son.

'What is the matter?' said she.

'Madame,' asked the man of quick execution, 'this child, is he the fruit of my loins, or those of Savoisy, your lover?'

At this question Bonne turned pale, and sprang upon her son like a frightened frog leaping into the water.

'Ah, he is really ours,' said she.

'If you do not wish to see his head roll at your feet confess yourself to me, and no prevarication. You have given me a lieutenant.'

'Indeed!'

'Who is he?'

'It is not Savoisy, and I will never say the name of a man that I don't know.'

Thereupon the constable rose, took his wife by the arm to cut her speech with a blow of the sword, but she, casting upon him an imperial glance, cried—

'Kill me if you will, but touch me not.'

'You shall live,' replied the husband, 'because I reserve you for a chastisement more ample than death.'

And doubting the inventions, snares, arguments, and artifices familiar to women in these desperate situations, of which they study night and day the variations, by themselves, or between themselves, he departed with this rude and bitter speech. He went instantly to interrogate his servants, presenting to them a face divinely terrible; so all of them replied to him as they would to God the Father on the Judgment Day, when each of us will be called to his account.

None of them knew the serious mischief which was at the bottom of these summary interrogations and crafty interlocutions; but from all that they said, the constable came to the conclusion that no male in his house was in the business, except one of his dogs, whom he found dumb, and to whom he had given the post of watching the gardens; so taking him in his hands, he strangled him with rage. This fact incited him by induction to suppose that the other constable came into his house by the garden, of which the only entrance was a postern opening on to the water side.

It is necessary to explain to those who are ignorant of it, the locality of the Hotel d'Armagnac, which had a notable situation near to the royal houses of St. Pol. On this site has since been built the hotel of Longueville. Then as at the present time, the residence of d'Armagnac had a porch of fine stone in Rue St. Antoine, was fortified at all points, and the high walls by the river side, in face of the Ile du Vaches, in the part where now stands the port of La Greve, were furnished with little towers. The design of these has for a long time been shown at the house of Cardinal Duprat, the king's Chancellor. The constable ransacked his brains, and at the bottom, from his finest stratagems, drew the best, and fitted it so well to the present case, that the gallant would be certain to be taken like a hare in the trap. "Sdeath,' said he, 'my planter of horns is taken, and I have the time now to think how I shall finish him off.'

Now this is the order of battle which this grand hairy captain who waged such glorious war against Duke Jean-sans-Peur commanded for the assault of his secret enemy. He took a goodly number of his most loyal and adroit archers, and placed them on the quay tower, ordering them under the heaviest penalties to draw without distinction of persons, except his wife, on those of his household who should attempt to leave the gardens, and to admit therein, either by night or by day, the favoured gentleman. The same was done on the porch side, in the Rue St. Antoine.

The retainers, even the chaplain, were ordered not to leave the house under pain of death. Then the guard of the two sides of the hotel having been committed to the soldiers of a company of ordnance, who were ordered to keep a sharp lookout in the side streets, it was certain that the unknown lover to whom the constable was indebted for his pair of horns, would be taken warm, when, knowing nothing, he should come at the accustomed hour of love to insolently plant his standard in the heart of the legitimate appurtenances of the said lord count.

It was a trap into which the most expert man would fall unless he was seriously protected by the fates, as was the good St. Peter by the Saviour when he prevented him going to the bottom of the sea the day when they had a fancy to try if the sea were as solid as terra firma.

The constable had business with the inhabitants of Poissy, and was obliged to be in the saddle after dinner, so that, knowing his intention, the poor Countess Bonne determined at night to invite her young gallant to that charming duel in which she was always the stronger.

While the constable was making round his hotel a girdle of spies and of death, and hiding his people near the postern to seize the gallant as he came out, not knowing where he would spring from, his wife was not amusing herself by threading peas nor seeking black cows in the embers. First, the maid-servant who had been stuck, unstuck herself and dragged herself to her mistress; she told her that her outraged lord knew nothing, and that before giving up the ghost she would comfort her dear mistress by assuring her that she could have perfect confidence in her sister, who was laundress in the hotel, and was willing to let herself be chopped up as small as sausage-meat to please Madame. That she was the most adroit and roguish woman in the neighbourhood, and renowned from the council chamber to the Trahoir cross among the common people, and fertile in invention for the desperate cases of love.

Then, while weeping for the decease of her good chamber woman, the countess sent for the laundress, made her leave her tubs and join her in rummaging the bag of good tricks, wishing to save Savoisy, even at the price of her future salvation.

First of all the two women determined to let him know their lord and master's suspicion, and beg him to be careful.

Now behold the good washerwoman who, carrying her tub like a mule, attempts to leave the hotel. But at the porch she found a man-at-arms who turned a deaf ear to all the blandishments of the wash-tub. Then she resolved, from her great devotion, to take the soldier on his weak side, and she tickled him so with her fondling that he romped very well with her, although he was armour-plated ready for battle; but when the game was over he still refused to let her go into the street and although she tried to get herself a passport sealed by some of the handsomest, believing them more gallant: neither the archers, men-at-arms, nor others, dared open for her the smallest entrance of the house. 'You are wicked and ungrateful wretches,' said she, 'not to render me a like service.'

Luckily at this employment she learned everything, and came back in great haste to her mistress, to whom she recounted the strange machinations of the count. The two women held a fresh council and had not considered, the time it takes to sing Alleluia, twice, these warlike appearances, watches, defences, and equivocal, specious, and diabolical orders and dispositions before they recognized by the sixth sense with which all females are furnished, the special danger which threatened the poor lover.

Madame having learned that she alone had leave to quit the house, ventured quickly to profit by her right, but she did not go the length of a bow-shot, since the constable had ordered four of his pages to be always on duty ready to accompany the countess, and two of the ensigns of his company not to leave her. Then the poor lady returned to her chamber, weeping as much as all the Magdalens one sees in the church pictures, could weep together.

'Alas!' said she, 'my lover must then be killed, and I shall never see him again!...he whose words were so sweet, whose manners were so graceful, that lovely head that had so often rested on my knees, will now be bruised... What! Can I not throw to my husband an empty and valueless head in place of the one full of charms and worth...a rank head for a sweet-smelling one; a hated head for a head of love.'

'Ah, Madame!' cried the washerwoman, 'suppose we dress up in the garments of a nobleman, the steward's son who is mad for me, and wearies me much, and having thus accoutered him, we push him out through the postern.

Thereupon the two women looked at each other with assassinating eyes.

'This marplot,' said she, 'once slain, all those soldiers will fly away like geese.'

'Yes, but will not the count recognize the wretch?'

And the countess, striking her breast, exclaimed, shaking her head, 'No, no, my dear, here it is noble blood that must be spilt without stint.'

Then she thought a little, and jumping with joy, suddenly kissed the laundress, saying, 'Because I have saved my lover's life by your counsel, I will pay you for his life until death.'

Thereupon the countess dried her tears, put on the face of a bride, took her little bag and a prayer-book, and went towards the Church of St. Pol whose bells she heard ringing, seeing that the last Mass was about to be said. In this sweet devotion the countess never failed, being a showy woman, like all the ladies of the court. Now this was called the full-dress Mass, because none but fops, fashionables, young gentlemen and ladies puffed out and highly scented, were to be met there. In fact no dresses was seen there without armorial bearings, and no spurs that were not gilt.

So the Countess of Bonne departed, leaving at the hotel the laundress much astonished, and charged to keep her eyes about her, and came with great pomp to the church, accompanied by her pages, the two ensigns and men-at-arms. It is here necessary to say that among the band of gallant knights who frisked round the ladies in church, the countess had more than one whose joy she was, and who had given his heart to her, after the fashion of youths who put down enough and to spare upon their tablets, only in order to make a conquest of at least one out of a great number.

Among these birds of fine prey who with open beaks looked oftener between the benches and the paternosters than towards the altar and the priests, there was one upon whom the countess sometimes bestowed the charity of a glance, because he was less trifling and more deeply smitten than all the others.

This one remained bashful, always stuck against the same pillar, never moving from it, but readily ravished with the sight alone of this lady whom he had chosen as his. His pale face was softly melancholy. His physiognomy gave proof of fine heart, one of those which nourish ardent passions and plunge delightedly into the despairs of love without hope. Of these people there are few, because ordinarily one likes more a certain thing than the unknown felicities lying and flourishing at the bottommost depths of the soul.

This said gentleman, although his garments were well made, and clean and neat, having even a certain amount of taste shown in the arrangement, seemed to the constable's wife to be a poor knight seeking fortune, and come from afar, with his nobility for his portion. Now partly from a suspicion of his secret poverty, partly because she was well beloved by him and a little because he had a good countenance, fine black hair, and a good figure, and remained humble and submissive in all, the constable's wife desired for him the favour of women and of fortune, not to let his gallantry stand idle, and from a good housewifely idea, she fired his imagination according to her fantasies, by certain small favours and little looks which serpented towards him like biting adders, trifling with the happiness of this young life, like a princess accustomed to play with objects more precious than a simple knight. In fact, her husband risked the whole kingdom as you would a penny at piquet. Finally it was only three days since, at the conclusion of vespers, that the constable's wife pointed out to the queen this follower of love, said laughingly—

'There's a man of quality.'

This sentence remained in the fashionable language. Later it became a custom so to designate the people of the court. It was to the wife of the constable d'Armagnac, and to no other source, that the French language is indebted for this charming expression.

By a lucky chance the countess had surmised correctly concerning this gentleman. He was a bannerless knight, named Julien de Boys-Bourredon, who not having inherited on his estate enough to make a toothpick, and knowing no other wealth than the rich nature with which his dead mother had opportunely furnished him, conceived the idea of deriving therefrom both rent and profit at court, knowing how fond ladies are of those good revenues, and value them high and dear, when they can stand being looked at between two suns. There are many like him who have thus taken the narrow road of women to make their way; but he, far from arranging his love in measured qualities, spend funds and all, as soon as he came to the full-dress Mass, he saw the triumphant beauty of the Countess Bonne. Then he fell really in love, which was a grand thing for his crowns, because he lost both thirst and appetite. This love is of the worst kind, because it incites you to the love of diet, during the diet of love; a double malady, of which one is sufficient to extinguish a man.

Such was the young gentlemen of whom the good lady had thought, and towards whom she came quickly to invite him to his death.

On entering she saw the poor chevalier, who faithful to his pleasure, awaited her, his back against a pillar, as a sick man longs for the sun, the spring-time, and the dawn. Then she turned away her eyes, and wished to go to the queen and request her assistance in this desperate case, for she took pity on her lover, but one of the captains said to her, with great appearance of respect, 'Madame, we have orders not to allow you to speak with man or woman, even though it should be the queen or your confessor. And remember that the lives of all of us are at stake.'

'Is it not your business to die?' said she.

'And also to obey,' replied the soldier.

Then the countess knelt down in her accustomed place, and again regarding her faithful slave, found his face thinner and more deeply lined than ever it had been.

'Bah!' said she, 'I shall have less remorse for his death; he is half dead as it is.'

With this paraphrase of her idea, she cast upon the said gentleman one of those warm ogles that are only allowable to princesses and harlots, and the false love which her lovely eyes bore witness to, gave a pleasant pang to the gallant of the pillar. Who does not love the warm attack of life when it flows thus round the heart and engulfs everything?

Madame recognized with a pleasure, always fresh in the minds of women, the omnipotence of her magnificent regard by the answer which, without saying a word, the chevalier made to it. And in fact, the blushes which empurpled his cheeks spoke better than the best speeches of the Greek and Latin orators, and were well understood. At this sweet sight, the countess, to make sure that it was not a freak of nature, took pleasure in experimentalizing how far the virtue of her eyes would go, and after having heated her slave more than thirty times, she was confirmed in her belief that he would bravely die for her. This idea so touched her, that from three repetitions between her orisons she was tickled with the desire to put into a lump all the joys of man, and to dissolve them for him in one single glance of love, in order that she should not one day be reproached with having not only dissipated the life, but also the happiness of this gentleman. When the officiating priest turned round to sing the Off you go to this fine gilded flock, the constable's wife went out by the side of the pillar where her courtier was, passed in front of him and endeavoured to insinuate into his understanding by a speaking glance that he was to follow her, and to make positive the intelligence and significant interpretation of this gentle appeal, the artful jade turned round again a little after passing him to again request his company. She saw that he had moved a little from his place, and dared not advance, so modest was he, but upon this last sign, the gentleman, sure of not being over-credulous, mixed with the crowd with little and noiseless steps, like an innocent who is afraid of venturing into one of those good places people call bad ones. And whether he walked behind or in front, to the right or to the left, my lady bestowed upon him a glistening glance to allure him the more and the better to draw him to her, like a fisher who gently jerks the lines in order to hook the gudgeon. To be brief: the countess practised so well the profession of the daughters of pleasure when they work to bring grist into their mills, that one would have said nothing resembled a harlot so much as a woman of high birth. And indeed, on arriving at the porch of her hotel the countess hesitated to enter therein, and again turned her face towards the poor chevalier to invite him to accompany her, discharging at him so diabolical a glance, that he ran to the queen of his heart, believing himself to be called by her. Thereupon, she offered him her hand, and both boiling and trembling from the contrary causes found themselves inside the house. At this wretched hour, Madame d'Armagnac was ashamed of having done all these harlotries to the profit of death, and of betraying Savoisy the better to save him; but this slight remorse was lame as the greater, and came tardily. Seeing everything ready, the countess leaned heavily upon her vassal's arm, and said to him—

'Come quickly to my room; it is necessary that I should speak with you.'

And he, not knowing that his life was in peril, found no voice wherewith to reply, so much did the hope of approaching happiness choke him.

When the laundress saw this handsome gentleman so quickly hooked, 'Ah!' said she, 'these ladies of the court are best at such work.' Then she honoured this courtier with a profound salutation, in which was depicted the ironical respect due to those who have the great courage to die for so little.

'Picard,' said the constable's lady, drawing the laundress to her by the skirt, 'I have not the courage to confess to him the reward with which I am about to pay his silent love and his charming belief in the loyalty of women.'

'Bah! Madame: why tell him? Send him away well contented by the postern. So many men die in war for nothing, cannot this one die for something? I'll produce another like him if that will console you.'

'Come along,' cried the countess, 'I will confess all to him. That will be the punishment for my sins.'

Thinking that this lady was arranging with her servant certain trifling provisions and secret things in order not to be disturbed in the interview she had promised him, the unknown lover kept at a discreet distance, looking at the flies. Nevertheless, he thought that the countess was very bold, but also, as even a hunchback would have done, he found a thousand reasons to justify her, and thought himself quite worthy to inspire such recklessness. He was lost in those good thoughts when the constable's wife opened the door of her chamber, and invited the chevalier to follow her in. There his noble lady cast aside all the apparel of her lofty fortune, and falling at the feet of this gentleman, became a simple woman.

'Alas, sweet sir!' said she, 'I have acted vilely towards you. Listen. On your departure from this house, you will meet your death. The love which I feel for another has bewildered me, and without being able to hold his place here, you will have to take it before his murderers. This is the joy to which I have bidden you.'

'Ah!' Replied Boys-Bourredon, interring in the depths of his heart a dark despair, 'I am grateful to you for having made use of me as of something which belonged to you... Yes, I love you so much that every day I have dreamed of offering you in imitation of the ladies, a thing that can be given but once. Take, then, my life!'

And the poor chevalier, in saying this, gave her one glance to suffice for all the time he would have been able to look at her through the long days. Hearing these brave and loving words,

Bonne rose suddenly.

'Ah! were it not for Savoisy, how I would love thee!' said she.

'Alas! my fate is then accomplished,' replied Boys-Bourredon. 'My horoscope predicted that I should die by the love of a great lady. Ah, God!' said he, clutching his good sword, 'I will sell my life dearly, but I shall die content in thinking that my decease ensures the happiness of her I love. I should live better in her memory than in reality.' At the sight of the gesture and the beaming face of this courageous man, the constable's wife was pierced to the heart. But soon she was wounded to the quick because he seemed to wish to leave her without even asking of her the smallest favour.

'Come, that I may arm you,' said she to him, making an attempt to kiss him.

'Ha! My lady-love,' replied he, moistening with a gentle tear the fire of his eyes, 'would you render my death impossible by attaching too great a value to my life?'

'Come,' cried she, overcome by this intense love, 'I do not know what the end of all this will be, but come—afterwards we will go and perish together at the postern.'

The same flame leaped in their hearts, the same harmony had struck for both, they embraced each other with a rapture in the delicious excess of that mad fever which you know well I hope; they fell into a profound forgetfulness of the dangers of Savoisy, of themselves, of the constable, of death, of life, of everything.

Meanwhile the watchman at the porch had gone to inform the constable of the arrival of the gallant, and to tell him how the infatuated gentleman had taken no notice of the winks which, during Mass and on the road, the countess had given him in order to prevent his destruction. They met their master arriving in great haste at the postern, because on their side the archers of the quay had whistled to him afar off, saying to him—

'The Sire de Savoisy has passed in.'

And indeed Savoisy had come at the appointed hour, and like

all the lovers, thinking only of his lady, he had not seen the count's spies and had slipped in at the postern. This collision of lovers was the cause of the constable's cutting short the words of those who came from the Rue St. Antoine, saying to them with a gesture of authority, that they did not think wise to disregard—

'I know that the animal is taken.'

Thereupon all rushed with a great noise through this said postern, crying, 'Death to him! Death to him!' and men-at-arms, archers, the constable, and the captains, all rushed full tilt upon Charles Savoisy, the king's nephew, who they attacked under the countess window, where by a strange chance, the groans of the poor young man were dolorously exhaled, mingled with the yells of the soldiers, at the same time as passionate sighs and cries were given forth by the two lovers, who hastened up in great fear.

'Ah!' said the countess, turning pale from terror, 'Savoisy is dying for me!'

'But I will live for you,' replied Boys-Bourredon, 'and shall esteem it a joy to pay the same price for my happiness as he has done.'

'Hide yourself in the clothes chest,' cried the countess; 'I hear the constable's footsteps.'

And indeed M. d'Armagnac appeared very soon with a head in his hand, and putting it all bloody on the mantleshelf, 'Behold, Madame,' said he, 'a picture which will enlighten you concerning the duties of a wife towards her husband.'

'You have killed an innocent man,' replied the countess, without changing colour. Savoisy was not my lover.'

And with the this speech she looked proudly at the constable with a face marked by so much dissimulation and feminine audacity, that the husband stood looking as foolish as a girl who has allowed a note to escape her below, before a numerous company, and he was afraid of having made a mistake.

'Of whom were you thinking this morning?' asked he.

'I was dreaming of the king,' said she.

'Then, my dear, why not have told me so?'

'Would you have believed me in the bestial passion you were in?'

The constable scratched his ear and replied—

'But how came Savoisy with the key of the postern?'

'I don't know,' she said, curtly, 'if you will have the goodness to believe what I have said to you.'

And his wife turned lightly on her heel like a weather-cock turned by the wind, pretending to go and look after the household affairs. You can imagine that d'Armagnac was greatly embarrassed with the head of poor Savoisy, and that for his part Boys-Bourredon had no desire to cough while listening to the count, who was growling to himself all sorts of words. At length the constable struck two heavy blows over the table and said, 'I'll go and attack the inhabitants of Poissy.' Then he departed, and when the night was come Boys-Bourredon escaped from the house in some disguise or other.

Poor Savoisy was sorely lamented by his lady, who had done all that a woman could do to save her lover, and later he was more than wept, he was regretted; for the countess having related this adventure to Queen Isabella, her majesty seduced Boys-Bourredon from the service of her cousin and put him to her own, so much was she touched with the qualities and firm courage of this gentleman.

Boys-Bourredon was a man whom danger had well recommended to the ladies. In fact he comported himself so proudly in everything in the lofty fortune, which the queen had made for him, that having badly treated King Charles one day when the poor man was in his proper senses, the courtiers, jealous of favour, informed the king of his cuckoldom. Boys-Bourredon was in a moment sewn in a sack and thrown into the Seine, near the ferry at Charenton, as everyone knows. I have no need add, that since the day when the constable took it into his head to play thoughtlessly with knives, his good wife utilized so well the two deaths he had caused and threw them so often in his face, that she made him as soft as a cat's paw and put him in the straight road of marriage; and he proclaimed her a modest and virtuous constable's lady, as indeed she was. As this book should, according to the maxims of great ancient authors, join certain useful things to the good laughs which you will find therein and contain precepts of high taste, I beg to inform you that the quintessence of the story is this: that women need never lose their heads in serious cases, because the God of Love never abandons them, especially when they are beautiful, young, and of good family; and that gallants when going to keep an amorous assignation should never go there like giddy young men, but carefully, and keep a sharp look-out near the burrow, to avoid falling into certain traps and to preserve themselves; for after a good woman the most precious thing is, certes, a pretty gentleman.

2

THE BROTHERS-IN-ARMS

At the commencement of the reign of King Henry, second of the name, who loved so well the fair Diana, there existed still a ceremony of which the usage has since become much weakened, and which has altogether disappeared, like an infinity of the good things of the olden times. This fine and noble custom was the choice which all knights made of a brother-in-arms. After having recognised each other as two loyal and brave men, each one of this pretty couple was married for life to the other; both became brothers, the one had to defend the other in battling against the enemies who threatened him, and at Court against the friends who slandered him. In the absence of his companion the other was expected to say to one who should have accused his good brother of any disloyalty, wickedness or dark felony, 'You have lied by your throat,' and so go into the field instantly, so sure was the one of the honour of the other. There is no need to add, that the one was always the second of the other in all affairs, good or evil, and that they shared all good or evil fortune. They were better than the brothers who are only united by the hazard of nature, since they were fraternized by the bonds of an especial sentiment, involuntary and mutual, and thus the fraternity of arms has produced splendid characters, as brave as those of the ancient Greeks, Romans, or others... But this is not my subject; the history of these things has been written by the historians of our country, and everyone knows them.

Now at this time two young gentlemen of Touraine, of whom one was the Cadet of Maille, and the other Sieur de Lavalliere, became brothers-in-arms on the day they gained their spurs. They were leaving the house of Monsieur de Montmorency, where they had been nourished with the good doctrines of this great Captain, and had shown how contagious is valour in such good company, for at the battle of Ravenna they merited the praises of the oldest knights. It was in the thick of this fierce fight that Maille, saved by the said Lavalliere, with whom he had had a quarrel or two, perceived that this gentleman had a noble heart. As they had each received slashes in the doublets, they baptised their fraternity with their blood, and were ministered to together in one and the same bed under the tent of Monsieur de Montmorency their master. It is necessary to inform you that, contrary to the custom of his family, which was always to have a pretty face, the Cadet of Maille was not of a pleasing physiognomy, and had scarcely any beauty but that of the devil. For the rest he was lithe as a greyhound, broad shouldered and strongly built as King Pepin, who was a terrible antagonist. On the other hand, the Sieur de Lavalliere was a dainty fellow, for whom seemed to have been invented rich laces, silken hose, and cancellated shoes. His long dark locks were pretty as a lady's ringlets, and he was, to be brief, a child with whom all the women would be glad to play. One day the Dauphine, niece of the Pope, said laughingly to the Queen of Navarre, who did not dislike these little jokes, 'that this page was a plaster to cure every ache', which caused the pretty little Tourainian to blush, because, being only sixteen, he took this gallantry as a reproach.

Now on his return from Italy the Cadet of Maille found the slipper of marriage ready for his foot, which his mother had obtained for him in the person of Mademoiselle d'Annebaut, who was a graceful maiden of good appearance, and well furnished with everything, having a splendid hotel in the Rue Barbette, with handsome furniture and Italian paintings and many considerable lands to inherit. Some days after the death of King Francis—a circumstance which planted terror in the heart of everyone, because his said Majesty had died in consequence of an attack of the Neapolitan sickness, and that for the future there would be no security even with princesses of the highest birth—the above-named Maille was compelled to quit the Court in order to go and arrange certain affairs of great importance in Piedmont. You may be sure that he was very loath to leave his good wife, so young, so delicate, so sprightly, in the midst of the dangers, temptations, snares and pitfalls of this gallant assemblage, which comprised so many handsome fellows, bold as eagles, proud of mein, and as fond of women as the people are partial to Paschal hams. In this state of intense jealousy everything made him ill at ease; but by dint of much thinking, it occurred to him to make sure of his wife in the manner about to be related. He invited his good brother-in-arms to come at daybreak on the morning of his departure. Now directly he heard Lavalliere's horse in the courtyard, he leaped out of bed, leaving his sweet and fair better-half sleeping that gentle, dreamy, dozing sleep so beloved by dainty ladies and lazy people. Lavalliere came to him, and the two companions, hidden in the embrasure of the window, greeted each other with a loyal clasp of the hand, and immediately Lavalliere said to Maille—

'I should have been here last night in answer to thy summons, but I had a love suit on with my lady, who had given me an assignation; I could in no way fail to keep it, but I quitted her at dawn. Shall I accompany thee? I have told her of thy departure, she has promised me to remain without any amour; we have made a compact. If she deceives me—well a friend is worth more than a mistress!'

'Oh! my good brother' replied Maille, quite overcome with these words, 'I wish to demand of thee a still higher proof of thy brave heart. Wilt thou take charge of my wife, defend her against all, be her guide, keep her in check and answer to me for the integrity of my head? Thou canst stay here during my absence, in the green-room, and be my wife's cavalier.'

Lavalliere knitted his brow and said—

'It is neither thee nor thy wife that I fear, but evil-minded people, who will take advantage of this to entangle us like skeins of silk.'

'Do not be afraid of me,' replied Maille, clasping Lavalliere to his breast. 'If it be the divine will of the Almighty that I should have the misfortune to be a cuckold, I should be less grieved if it were to your advantage. But by my faith I should die of grief, for my life is bound up in my good, young, virtuous wife.'

Saying which, he turned away his head, in order that Lavalliere should not perceive the tears in his eyes; but the fine courtier saw this flow of water, and taking the hand of Maille—

'Brother,' said he to him, 'I swear to thee on my honour as a man, that before anyone lays a finger on thy wife, he shall have felt my dagger in the depth of his veins! And unless I should die, thou shalt find her on thy return, intact in body if not in heart, because thought is beyond the control of gentlemen.'

'It is then decreed above,' exclaimed Maille, 'that I shall always be thy servant and thy debtor!'

Thereupon the comrade departed, in order not to be inundated with the tears, exclamations, and other expressions of grief which ladies make use of when saying 'Farewell'. Lavalliere having conducted him to the gate of the town, came back to the hotel, waited until Marie d'Annebaut was out of bed, informed her of the departure of her good husband, and offered to place himself at her orders, in such a graceful manner, that the most virtuous woman would have been tickled with a desire to keep such a knight to herself. But there was no need of this fine paternoster to indoctrinate the lady, seeing that she had listened to the discourse of the two friends, and was greatly offended at her husband's doubt. Alas! God alone is perfect! In all the ideas of men there is always a bad side, and it is therefore a great science in life, but an impossible science, to take hold of everything, even a stick by the right end. The cause of the great difficulty there is in pleasing the ladies is, that there is it in them a thing which is more woman than they are, and but for the respect which is due to them, I would use another word. Now we should never awaken the phantasy of this malevolent thing. The perfect government of woman is a task to rend a man's heart, and we are compelled to remain in perfect submission to them; that is, I imagine, the best manner in which to solve the most agonizing enigma of marriage.

Now Marie d'Annebaut was delighted with the bearing and offers of this gallant; but there was something in her smile which indicated a malicious idea, and, to speak plainly, the intention of putting her young guardian between honour and pleasure; to regale him so with love, to surround him with so many little attentions, to pursue him with such warm glances, that he would be faithless to friendship, to the advantage of gallantry.

Everything was in perfect trim for the carrying out of her design, because of the companionship which the Sire de Lavalliere would be obliged to have with her during his stay in the hotel, and as there is nothing in the world can turn a woman from her whim, at every turn the artful jade was ready to catch him in a trap.

At times she would make him remain seated near her by the fire, until twelve o'clock at night, singing soft refrains, and at every opportunity showed her fair shoulders, and the white temptations of which her corset was full, and casting upon him a thousand piercing glances, all without showing in her face the thoughts that surged in her brain.

At times she would walk with him in the morning, in the gardens of the hotel, leaning heavily upon his arm, pressing it, sighing, and making him tie the laces of her little shoes, which were always coming undone in that particular place. Then it would be those soft words and things which the ladies understand so well, little attentions paid to a guest, such as coming in to see if he were comfortable, if his bed were well made, the room clean, if the ventilation were good, if he felt any draughts in the night, if the sun came in during the day, and asking him to forgo none of his usual fancies and habits, saying—

'Are you accustomed to take anything in the morning in bed, such as honey, milk, or spice? Do the meal times suit you? I will conform mine to yours: tell me. You are afraid to ask me. Come—'

She accompanied these coddling little attentions with a hundred affected speeches; for instance, on coming into the room she would say—

'I am intruding, send me away. You want to be left alone—I will go.' And always was she graciously invited to remain.

And the cunning Madame always came lightly attired, showing samples of her beauty, which would have made a patriarch neigh, even were he as much battered by time as must have been Mr Methusaleh, with his nine hundred and sixty years.

That good knight being as sharp as a needle, let the lady go on with her tricks, much pleased to see her occupy herself with him, since it was so much gained; but like a loyal brother, he always called her absent husband to the lady's mind.

Now one evening—the day had been very warm—Lavalliere suspecting the lady's games, told her that Maille loved her dearly, that she had in him a man of honour, a gentleman who doted on her, and was ticklish on the score of his crown.

'Why then, if he is so ticklish in this manner, has he placed you here?'

'Was it not a most prudent thing?' replied he. 'Was it not necessary to confide you to some defender of your virtue? Not that it needs one save to protect you from wicked men.'

'Then you are my guardian?' said she.

'I am proud of it!' exclaimed Lavalliere.

'Ah!' said she, 'he has made a very bad choice.'

This remark was accompanied by a little look, so lewdly lascivious that the good brother-in-arms put on, by way of reproach, a severe countenance, and left the fair lady alone, much piqued at this refusal to commence love's conflict.

She remained in deep meditation, and began to search for the real obstacle that she had encountered, for it was impossible that it should enter the mind of any lady, that a gentleman could despise that bagatelle which is of such great price and so high value. Now these thoughts knitted and joined together so well, one fitting into the other, that out of little pieces she constructed a perfect whole, and found herself desperately in love; which should teach the ladies never to play with a man's weapons, seeing that like glue, they always stick to the fingers.

By this means Marie d'Annebaut came to a conclusion which she should have known at the commencement—viz., that to keep clear of her snares, the good knight must be smitten with some other lady, and looking round her, to see where her young guest could have found a needle-case to his taste, she thought of the fair Limeuil, one of Queen Catherine's maids, of Mesdames de Nevers, d'Estree, and de Giac, all of whom were declared friends of Lavalliere, and of the lot he must love one to distraction.

From this belief, she added the motive of jealousy to the others which tempted her to seduce her Argus, whom she did not wish to wound, but to perfume, kiss his head, and treat kindly.

She was certainly more beautiful, young, and more appetizing and gentle than her rivals; at least, that was the melodious decree of her imaginations. So, urged on by the chords and springs of conscience, and physical causes which affect women, she returned to the charge, to commence a fresh assault upon the heart of the chevalier, for the ladies like that which is well fortified.

Then she played the pussy-cat, and nestled up close to him,

became so sweetly sociable, and wheedled so gently, that one evening when she was in a desponding state, although merry enough in her inmost soul, the guardian-brother asked her—

'What is the matter with you?'

To which she replied to him dreamily, being listened to by him as the sweetest music—

That she had married Maille against her heart's will, and that she was very unhappy; that she knew not the sweets of love; that her husband did not understand her, and that her life was full of tears. In fact, that she was a maiden in heart and all, since she confessed in marriage she had experienced nothing but the reverse of pleasure. And she added, that surely this holy state should be full of sweetmeats and dainties of love, because all the ladies hurried into it, and hated and were jealous of those who out-bid them, for it cost certain people pretty dear; that she was so curious about it that for one good day or night of love, she would give her life, and always be obedient to her lover without a murmur; but that he with whom she would sooner than all others try the experiment would not listen to her; that, nevertheless, the secret of their love might be kept eternally, so great was her husband's confidence in him, and that finally if he still refused it would kill her.

And all these paraphrases of the common canticle known to the ladies at their birth were ejaculated between a thousand pauses, interrupted with sighs torn from the heart, ornamented with quiverings, appeals to heaven, upturned eyes, sudden blushings and clutchings at her hair. In fact, no ingredient of temptation was lacking in the dish, and at the bottom of all these words there was a nipping desire which embellished even its blemishes. The good knight fell at the lady's feet, and weeping took them and kissed them, and you may be sure the good woman was quite delighted to let him kiss them, and even without looking too carefully to see what she was going to do, she abandoned her dress to him, knowing well that to keep it from sweeping the ground it must be taken at the bottom to raise it; but it was written that for that evening she should be good, for the handsome Lavalliere said to her with despair—

'Ah, madame, I am an unfortunate man and a wretch.'

'Not at all,' said she.

'Alas, the joy of loving you is denied to me.'

'How?' said she.

'I dare not confess my situation to you!'

'Is it then very bad?'

'Ah, you will be ashamed of me!'

'Speak, I will hide my face in my hands,' and the cunning madame hid her face in such a way that she could look at her well-beloved between her fingers.

'Alas!' said he, 'the other evening when you addressed me in such gracious words, I was so treacherously inflamed, that not knowing my happiness to be so near, and not daring to confess my flame to you, I ran to a Bordel where all the gentleman go, and there for love of you, and to save the honour of my brother whose head I should blush to dishonour, I was so badly infected that I am in great danger of dying of the Italian sickness.'

The lady, seized with terror, gave vent to the cry of a woman in labour, and with great emotion, repulsed him with a gentle little gesture. Poor Lavalliere, finding himself in so pitiable a state, went out of the room, but he had not even reached the tapestries of the door, when Marie d'Annebaut again contemplated him, saying to herself, 'Ah! what a pity!' Then she fell into a state of great melancholy, pitying in herself the gentleman, and became the more in love with him because he was fruit three times forbidden.

'But for Maille,' said she to him, one evening that she thought him handsomer than unusual, 'I would willingly take your disease. Together we should then have the same terrors.'

'I love you too well,' said the brother, 'not to be good.'

And he left her to go to his beautiful Limeuil. You can imagine that being unable to refuse to receive the burning glances of the lady, during meal times, and the evenings, there was a fire nourished that warmed them both, but she was compelled to live without touching her cavalier, otherwise than with her eyes. Thus occupied, Marie d'Annebaut was fortified at every point against the gallants of the Court, for there are no bounds so impassable as those of love, and no better guardian; it is like the devil, he whom it has in its clutches it surrounds with flames. One evening, Lavalliere having escorted his friend's wife to a dance given by Queen Catherine, he danced with the fair Limeuil, with whom he was madly in love. At that time the knights carried on their amours bravely two by two, and even in troops. Now all the ladies were jealous of La Limeuil, who at that time was thinking of yielding to the handsome Lavalliere. Before taking their places in the quadrille, she had given him the sweetest of assignations for the morrow, during the hunt. Our great Queen Catherine, who from political motives fermented these loves and stirred them up, like pastrycooks make the oven fires burn by poking, glanced at all the pretty couples interwoven in the quadrille, and said to her husband—

'When they combat here, can they conspire against you, eh?'

'Ah! But the Protestants?'

'Bah! Have them here as well,' said she, laughing. 'Why, look at Lavalliere, who is suspected to be a Huguenot; he is converted by my dear little Limeuil, who does not play her cards badly for a young lady of sixteen. He will soon have her name down in his list.'

'Ah, Madame! Do not believe it,' said Marie d'Annebaut, 'he is ruined through that same sickness of Naples which made you queen.'

At this artless confession, Catherine, the fair Diana, and the king, who were sitting together, burst out laughing, and the thing ran round the room. This brought endless shame and mockery upon Lavalliere. The poor gentleman, pointed at by everyone, soon wished somebody else in his shoes, for La Limeuil, who his rivals had not been slow laughingly to warn of her danger, appeared to shrink from her lover, so rapid was the spread, and so violent the apprehensions of this nasty disease. Thus Lavalliere found himself abandoned by everyone like a leper. The king made an offensive remark, and the good knight quitted the ball-room, followed by poor Marie in despair at the speech. She had in every way ruined the man she loved: she had destroyed his honour, and marred his life, since the physicians and master surgeons advance as a fact, incapable of contradiction, that persons Italianized by this love sickness, lost through it their greatest attractions, as well as their generative powers, and their bones went black.

Thus no woman would bind herself in legitimate marriage with the finest gentlemen in the kingdom if he were only suspected of being one of those whom Master Frances Rabelais named 'his very precious scabby ones...'

As the handsome knight was very silent and melancholy, his companion said to him on the road home from Hercules House, where the fete had been held—

'My dear lord, I have done you a great mischief.'

'Ah, madame!' replied Lavalliere, 'My hurt is curable; but into what a predicament have you fallen? You should not have been aware of the danger of my love.'

'Ah!' said she, 'I am sure now always to have you to myself; in exchange for this great obloquy and dishonour, I will be forever your friend, your hostess, and your lady-love—more than that, your servant. My determination is to devote myself to you and efface the traces of this shame; to cure you by a watch and ward; and if the learned in these matters declare that the disease has such a hold of you that it will kill you like our defunct sovereign, I must still have your company in order to die gloriously in dying of your complaint. Even then,' said she, weeping, 'that will not be penance enough to atone for the wrong I have done you.'

These words were accompanied with big tears; her virtuous heart waxed faint, she fell to the ground exhausted. Lavalliere, terrified, caught her and placed his hand upon her heart, below a breast of matchless beauty. The lady revived at the warmth of this beloved hand, experiencing such exquisite delights as nearly to make her again unconscious.

'Alas!' said she, 'this sly and superficial caress will be for the future the only pleasure of our love. It will still be a hundred times better than the joys which poor Maille fancies he is bestowing on me... Leave your hand there,' said she; 'verily it is upon my soul, and touches it.'

At these words the knight was in a pitiful plight, and innocently confessed to the lady that he experienced so much pleasure at this touch that the pains of his malady increased, and that death was preferable to this martyrdom.

'Let us die then,' said she.

But the litter was in the courtyard of the hotel, and as the means of death was not handy, each one slept far from the other, heavily weighed down with love, Lavalliere having lost his fair Limeuil, and Marie d'Annebaut having gained pleasures without parallel.

From this affair, which was quite unforeseen, Lavalliere found himself under the ban of love and marriage and dared no longer appear in public, and he found how much it costs to guard the virtue of a woman; but the more honour and virtue he displayed the more pleasure did he experience in these great sacrifices offered at the shrine of brotherhood. Nevertheless, his duty was very bitter, very ticklish, and intolerable to perform, towards the last days of his guard. And in this way.

The confession of her love, which she believed was returned, the wrong done by her to her cavalier, and the experience of an unknown pleasure, emboldened the fair Marie, who fell into a platonic love, gently tempered with those little indulgences in which there is no danger. From this cause sprang the diabolical pleasures of the game invented by the ladies, who since the death of Francis the First feared the contagion, but wished to gratify their lovers. To these cruel delights, in order to properly play his part, Lavalliere could not refuse his sanction. Thus every evening the mournful Marie would attach her guest to her petticoats, holding his hand, kissing him with burning glances, her cheek placed gently against his, and during this virtuous embrace, in which the knight was held like the devil by a holy water brush, she told him of her great love, which was boundless since it stretched through the infinite spaces of unsatisfied desire. All the fire with which the ladies endow their substantial amours, when the night has no other lights than their eyes, she transferred into the mystic motions of her head, the exultations of her soul, and the ecstasies of her heart. Then, naturally, and with the delicious joy of two angels united by thought alone, they intoned together those sweet litanies repeated by the lovers of the period in honour of love—anthems which the abbot of Theleme has paragraphically saved from oblivion by engraving them on the walls of his Abbey, situated, according to master Alcofribas, in our land of Chinon, where I have seen them in Latin, and have translated them for the benefit of Christians.

'Alas!' said Marie d'Annebaut, 'Thou art my strength and my life, my joy and my treasure.'

'And you,' replied he, 'you are a pearl, an angel.'

'Thou art my seraphim.'

'You my soul.'

'Thou my God.'

'You my evening star and morning star, my honour, my beauty, my universe.'

'Thou my great my divine master.'

'You my glory, my faith, my religion.'

'Thou my gentle one, my handsome one, my courageous one, my dear one, my cavalier, my defender, my king, my love.'

'You my fairy, the flower of my days, the dream of my nights.'

'Thou my thought at every moment.'

'You the delights of my eyes.'

'Thou the voice of my soul.'

'You my light by day.'

'Thou my glimmer in the night.'

'You the best beloved among women.'

'Thou the most adored of men.'

'You my blood, a myself better than myself.'

'Thou art my heart, my lustre.'

'You my saint, my only joy.'

'I yield thee the palm of love, and how great so'er mine be, I believe thou lovest me still more, for thou art the lord.'

'No; the palm is yours, my goddess, my Virgin Marie.'

'No; I am thy servant, thine handmaiden, a nothing thou canst crush to atoms.'

'No, no! It is I who am your slave, your faithful page, whom you see as a breath of air, upon whom you can walk as on a carpet. My heart is your throne.'

'No, dearest, for thy voice transfigures me.'

'Your regard burns me.'

'I see but thee.'

'I love but you.'

'Oh! Put thine hand upon my heart—only thine hand—and thou will see me pale, when my blood shall have taken the heat of thine.'

Then during these struggles their eyes, already ardent, flamed still more brightly, and the good knight was a little the accomplice of the pleasure which Marie d'Annebaut took in feeling his hand upon her heart. Now, as in this light embrace all their strength was put forth, all their desires strained, all their ideas of the thing concentrated, it happened that the knight's transport reached a climax. Their eyes wept warm tears, they seized each other hard and fast as fire seizes houses; but that was all. Lavalliere had promised to return safe and sound to his friend the body only, not the heart.

When Maille announced his return, it was quite time, since no virtue could avoid melting upon this gridiron; and the less licence the lovers had, the more pleasure they had in their fantasies.

Leaving Marie d'Annebaut, the good companion in arms went as far as Bondy to meet his friend, to help him to pass through the forest without accident, and the two brothers slept together, according to the ancient custom, in the village of Bondy.

There, in their bed, they recounted to each other, one of the adventures of his journey, the other the gossip of the camp, stories of gallantry, and the rest. But Maille's first question was touching Marie d'Annebaut, whom Lavalliere swore to be intact in that precious place where the honour of husbands is lodged; at which the amorous Maille was highly delighted.

On the morrow, they were all three re-united, to the great disgust of Marie, who, with the high jurisprudence of women, made a great fuss with her good husband, but with her finger she indicated her heart in an artless manner to Lavalliere, as one who said, 'This is thine!'

At supper Lavalliere announced his departure for the wars. Maille was much grieved at this resolution, and wished to accompany his brother; that Lavalliere refused him point blank.

'Madame,' said he to Marie d'Annebaut, 'I love you more than life, but not more than honour.'

He turned pale saying this, and Madame de Maille blanched hearing him, because never in their amorous dalliance had there been so much true love as in this speech. Maille insisted on keeping his friend company as far as Meaux. When he came back he was talking over with his wife the unknown reasons and secret causes of this departure, when Marie, who suspected the grief of poor Lavalliere said, 'I know: he is ashamed to stop here because he has the Neapolitan sickness.'

'He!' said Maille, quite astonished. 'I saw him when we were in bed together at Bondy the other evening, and yesterday at Meaux. There's nothing the matter with him; he is as sound as a bell.'

The lady burst into tears, admiring this great loyalty, the sublime resignation to his oath, and the extreme sufferings of this internal passion. But as she still kept her love in the recesses of her heart, she died when Lavalliere fell before Metz, as has been elsewhere related by Messire Bourdeilles de Brantome in his tittle-tattle.

3

DESPAIR IN LOVE

At the time when King Charles the Eighth took it into his head to decorate the castle of Amboise, they came with him certain workmen, master sculptors, good painters, and masons, or architects, who ornamented the galleries with splendid works, which, through neglect, have since been much spoiled.

At that time the court was staying in this beautiful locality, and, as everyone knows, the king took great pleasure in watching his people work out their ideas. Among these foreign gentlemen was an Italian, named Angelo Cappara, a most worthy young man, and, in spite of his age, a better sculptor and engraver than any of them; and it astonished many to see one in the April of his life so clever. Indeed, there had scarcely sprouted upon his visage the hair which imprints upon a man virile majesty. To this Angelo the ladies took a great fancy because he was charming as a dream, and as melancholy as a dove left solitary in its nest by the death of its mate. And this was the reason thereof: this sculptor knew the curse of poverty, which mars and troubles all the actions of life; he lived miserably, eating little, ashamed of his pennilessness, and made use of his talents only through great despair, wishing by any means to win that idle life which is the best for all those whose minds are occupied. The Florentine, out of bravado, came to the court gallantly attired, and from the timidity of youth and misfortune dared not ask his money from the king, who, seeing him thus dressed, believed him well with everything. The courtiers and the ladies used all to admire his beautiful works, and also their author; but of money he got none. All, and the ladies above all, finding him rich by nature, esteemed him well off with his youth, his long black hair, and bright eyes, and did not give a thought to lucre, while thinking of these things and the rest. Indeed they were quite right, since these advantages gave to many a rascal of the court, lands, money and all. In spite of his youthful appearance, Master Angelo was twenty years of age, and no fool, had a large heart, a head full of poetry; and more than that, was a man of lofty imaginings. But although he had little confidence in himself, like all poor and unfortunate people, he was astonished at the success of the ignorant. He fancied that he was ill-fashioned, either in body or mind, and kept his thoughts to himself. I am wrong, for he told them in the clear starlight nights to the shadows, to God, to the devil, and everything about him. At such times he would lament his fate in having a heart so warm, that doubtless the ladies avoided him as they would a red-hot iron; then he would say to himself how he would worship a beautiful mistress, how all his life long he would honour her, and with what fidelity he would attach himself to her, with what affection serve her, how studiously obey her commands, with what sports he would dispel the light clouds of her melancholy sadness on the days when the skies should be overcast. Fashioning himself one out of his imagination, he would throw himself at her feet, kiss, fondle, caress, bite, and clasp her with as much reality as a prisoner scampers over the grass when he sees the green fields through the bars of his cell. Thus he would appeal to her mercy; overcome with his feelings, would stop her breath with his embraces, would become daring in spite of his respect, and passionately bite the clothes of his bed, seeking this celestial lady, full of courage when by himself, but abashed on the morrow if he passed one by. Nevertheless, inflamed by these amorous advances, he would hammer away anew at his marble figures, would carve beautiful breasts, to bring the water into one's mouth at the sight of those sweet fruits of love, without counting the other things that he raised, carved, and caressed with the chisels, smoothed down with his file, and fashioned in a manner that would make their use intelligible to the mind of a greenhorn, and stain his verdure in a single day. The ladies would criticize these beauties, and all of them were smitten with the youthful Cappara. And the youthful Cappara would eye them up and down, swearing that the day one of them gave him her little finger to kiss, he would have his desire.

Among these high-born ladies there came one day one by herself to the young Florentine, asking him why he was so shy, and if none of the court ladies could make him sociable. Then she graciously invited him to come to her house that evening.

Master Angelo perfumes himself, purchases a velvet mantle with a double fringe of satin, borrows from a friend a cloak with wide sleeves, a slashed doublet, and silken hose, arrives at the house, and ascends the stairs with hasty feet, hope beaming from his eyes, knowing not what to do with his heart, which leaped and bounded like a goat; and, to sum up, so much over head and ears in love, that the perspiration trickled down his back.

You may be sure the lady was beautiful, and Master Cappara was the more aware of it, since in his profession he had studied the mouldings of the arms, the lines of the body, the secret surroundings of the sex, and other mysteries. Now this lady satisfied the especial rules of art; and besides being fair and slender, she had a voice to disturb life in its source, to stir fire of a heart, brain, and everything; in short, she put into one's imagination delicious images of love without thinking of it, which is the characteristic of these cursed women.

The sculptor found her seated by the fire in a high chair, and the lady immediately commenced to converse at her ease, although Angelo could find no other replies than 'Yes' and 'No', could get no other words from his throat nor idea in his brain, and would have beaten his head against the fireplace but for the happiness of gazing at and listening to his lovely mistress, who was playing there like a young fly in the sunshine. Because, which this mute admiration, both remained until the middle of the night, wandering slowly down the flowery path of love, the good sculptor went away radiant with happiness. On the road, he concluded in his own mind, that if a noble lady kept him rather close to her skirts during four hours of the night, it would not matter a straw if she kept him there the remainder. Drawing from these premises certain corollaries, he resolved to ask her favours as a simple woman. Then he determined to kill everybody—the husband, the wife, or himself—rather than lose the distaff whereon to spin one hour of joy. Indeed, he was so mad with love, that he believed life to be but a small stake in the game of love, since one single day of it was worth a thousand lives.

The Florentine chiselled away at his statues, thinking of his evening, and thus spoiled many a nose thinking of something else. Noticing this, he left his work, perfumed himself, and went to listen to the sweet words of his lady, with the hope of turning them into deeds; but when he was in the presence of his sovereign, her feminine majesty made itself felt, and poor Cappara, such a lion in the street, looked sheepish when gazing at his victim. This notwithstanding, towards the hour when desire becomes heated, he was almost in the lady's lap and held her tightly clasped. He had obtained a kiss, had taken it, much to his delight; for, when they give it, the ladies retain the right of refusal, but when they left it to be taken, the lover may take a thousand. This is the reason why all of them are accustomed to let it be taken. The Florentine had stolen a great number, and things were going on admirably, when the lady, who had been thrifty with her favours, cried, 'My husband!'

And, in fact, my lord had just returned from playing tennis, and the sculptor had to leave the place, but not without receiving a warm glance from the lady interrupted in her pleasure. This was all his substance, pittance and enjoyment during a whole month, since on the brink of his joy always came the said husband, and he always arrived wisely between a point-blank refusal and those little sweet caresses with which women always season their refusals—little things which reanimate love and render it all the stronger. And when the sculptor, out of patience, commenced, immediately upon his arrival, the skirmish of the skirt, in order that victory might arrive before the husband, to whom, no doubt, these disturbances were not without profit, his fine lady, seeing desire written in the eyes of her sculptor, commenced endless quarrels and altercations; at first she pretended to be jealous in order to rail against love; then appeased the anger of the little one with the moisture of a kiss, then kept the conversation to herself, and kept on saying that her lover should be good, obedient to her will, otherwise she would not yield to him her life and soul; that a desire was a small thing to offer a mistress; that she was more courageous, because loving more she sacrificed more, and to his propositions she would exclaim, 'Silence, sir!' with the air of a queen, and at times she would put on an angry look, to reply to the reproachs of Cappara: 'If you are not as I wish you to be, I will no longer love you.'

The poor Italian saw, when it was too late, that this was not a noble love, one of those which does not mete out joy as a miser his crowns; and that this lady took delight in letting him jump about outside the hedge and be master of everything, provided he touched not the garden of love. At this business Cappara became a savage enough to kill anyone, and took with him trusty companions, his friends, to whom he gave the task of attacking the husband while walking home to bed after his game of tennis with the king. He came to his lady at the accustomed hour when the sweet sports of love were in full swing, which sports were long, lasting kisses, hair twisted and untwisted, hand bitten with passion, ears as well; indeed, the whole business, with the exception of that especial thing which good authors rightly find abominable. The Florentine exclaims between two hearty kisses—

'Sweet one, do you love me more than anything?'

'Yes,' said she, because words never cost anything.

'Well then,' replied the lover, 'be mine in deed as in word.'

'But,' said she, 'my husband will be here directly.'

'Is that the only reason?' said he.

'Yes.'

'I have friends who will cross him, and will not let him go unless I show a torch at this window. If he complain to the king, my friends will say, they thought they were playing a joke on one of their own set.'

'Ah, my dear,' said she, 'let me see if everyone in the house is gone to bed.'

She rose, and held the light to the window. Seeing which Cappara blew out the candle, seized his sword, and placing himself in front of the woman, whose scorn and evil mind he recognized.

'I will not kill you, madame,' said he, 'but I will mark your face in such a manner you will never again coquette with young lovers whose lives you waste. You have deceived me shamefully, and are not a respectable woman. You must know that a kiss will never sustain life in a true lover, and that a kissed mouth needs the rest. Your have made my life forever dull and wretched; now I will make you remember forever my death, which you have caused. You shall never again behold yourself in a glass without seeing there my face also.' Then he raised his arm, and held the sword ready to cut off a good slice of the fresh fair cheek, where still all the traces of his kiss remained. And the lady exclaimed, 'You wretch!'

'Hold your tongue,' said he; 'you told me that you loved me

better than anything. Now you say otherwise; each evening have you raised me a little nearer to heaven; with one blow you cast me into hell, and you think that your petticoat can save you from a lover's wrath—No!'

'Ah, my Angelo! I am thine,' said she, marvelling at this man glaring with rage.

But he, stepping three paces back, replied, 'Ah, woman of the court and wicked heart, thou lovest, then, thy face better than thy lover.'

She turned pale, and humbly held up her face, for she understood that at this moment her past perfidy wronged her present love. With a single blow Angelo slashed her face, then left her house, and quitted the country. The husband not having been stopped by reason of that light which was seen by the Florentines, found his wife minus her left cheek. But she spoke not a word in spite of her agony; she loved her Cappara more than life itself. Nevertheless, the husband wished to know whence preceded this wound. No one having been there except the Florentine, he complained to the king, who had his workman hastily pursued, and ordered him to be hanged at Blois. On the day of execution a noble lady was seized with a desire to save this courageous man, whom she believed to be a lover of the right sort. She begged the king to give him to her, which he did willingly. But Cappara declaring that he belonged entirely to his lady, the memory of whom he could not banish entirely, entered the Church, became a cardinal and a great savant, and used to say in his old age that he had existed upon the remembrance of the joys tasted in those poor hours of anguish; in which he was, at the same time, both very well and very badly treated by his lady. There are authors saying afterwards he succeeded better with his old sweetheart, whose cheek healed; but I cannot believe this, because he was a man of heart, who had a high opinion of the holy joys of love.

This teaches us nothing worth knowing, unless it be that there are unlucky meetings in life, since this tale is in every way true. If in other places the author has overshot the truth, this one will gain for him the indulgence of the conclave of lovers.

EPILOGUE

This second series comes in the merry month of June, when all is green and gay, because the poor muse, whose slave the author is, has been more capricious then the love of a queen, and has mysteriously wished to bring forth her fruit in the time of flowers. No one can boast himself master of this fay. At times, when grave thoughts occupy the mind and grieve the brain, comes the jade whispering her merry tales in the author's ear, tickling her lips with her feathers, dancing sarabands, and making the house echo with her laughter. If by chance the writer, abandoning science for pleasure, says to her, 'Wait a moment, little one, till I come,' and runs in great haste to play with the madcap, she has disappeared. She has gone into her hole, hides herself there, rolls herself up, and retires. Take the poker, take a staff, a cudgel, a cane, raise them, strike the wench, and rave at her, she moans; strap her, she moans; caress her, fondle her, she moans; kiss her, say to her, 'Here, little one,' she moans. Now she's cold, now she is going to die; adieu to love, adieu to laughter, adieu to merriment, adieu to good stories. Wear mourning for her, weep and fancy her dead, groan. Then she raises her head, her merry laugh rings out again; she spreads her white wings, flies one knows not wither, turns in the air, capers, shows her impish tail, her woman's breasts, her strong loins, and her angelic face, shakes her perfumed tresses, gambols in the rays of the sun, shines forth in all her beauty, changes her colours like the breast of a dove, laughs until she cries, cast the tears of her eyes into the sea, where the fishermen find them transmuted into pretty pearls, which are gathered to adorn the foreheads of queens. She twists about like a colt broken loose, exposing her virgin charms, and a thousand things so fair that a pope would peril his salvation for her at the mere sight of them. During these wild pranks of the ungovernable beast you meet fools and friends, who say to the poor poet, 'Here are your tales? Where are your new volumes? You are a pagan prognosticator. Oh yes, you are known. You go to fetes and feasts, and do nothing between your meals. Where's your work?'

Although I am by nature partial to kindness, I should like to see one of these people impaled in the Turkish fashion, and thus equipped, sent on the Love Chase. Here endeth the second series; make the devil give it a lift with his horns, and it will be well received by a smiling Christendom.

4

A PASSION IN THE DESERT

'The whole show is dreadful,' she cried coming out of the menagerie of M. Martin. She had just been looking at that daring speculator 'working with his hyena'—to speak in the style of the programme.

'By what means,' she continued, 'can he have tamed these animals to such a point as to be certain of their affection for—'

'What seems to you a problem,' said I, interrupting, 'is really quite natural.'

'Oh!' she cried, letting an incredulous smile wander over her lips.

'You think that beasts are wholly without passions?' I asked her. 'Quite the reverse; we can communicate to them all the vices arising in our own state of civilization.'

She looked at me with an air of astonishment.

'But,' I continued, 'the first time I saw M. Martin, I admit, like you, I did give vent to an exclamation of surprise. I found myself next to an old soldier with the right leg amputated, who had come in with me. His face had struck me. He had one of those heroic heads, stamped with the seal of warfare, and on which the battles of Napoleon are written. Besides, he had that frank, good-humoured expression which always impresses me favourably. He was without doubt one of those troopers who are surprised at nothing, who find matter for laughter in the contortions of a dying comrade, who bury or plunder him quite light-heartedly, who stand intrepidly in the way of bullets;—in fact, one of those men who waste no time in deliberation, and would not hesitate to make friends with the devil himself. After looking very attentively at the proprietor of the menagerie getting out of his box, my companion pursed up his lips with an air of mockery and contempt, with that peculiar and expressive twist which superior people assume to show they are not taken in. Then, when I was expatiating on the courage of M. Martin, he smiled, shook his head knowingly, and said, 'Well known.'

'How "well known"?' I said. 'If you would only explain me the mystery, I should be vastly obliged.'

'After a few minutes, during which we made acquaintance, we went to dine at the first restauranteur's whose shop caught our eye. At dessert a bottle of champagne completely refreshed and brightened up the memories of this odd old soldier. He told me his story, and I saw that he was right when he exclaimed, "Well known."'

When she got home, she teased me to that extent, was so charming, and made so many promises, that I consented to communicate to her the confidences of the old soldier. Next day she received the following episode of an epic which one might call 'The French in Egypt'.

During the expedition in Upper Egypt under General Desaix, a Provencal soldier fell into the hands of the Maugrabins, and was taken by these Arabs into the deserts beyond the falls of the Nile.

In order to place a sufficient distance between themselves and the French army, the Maugrabins made forced marches, and only halted when night was upon them. They camped round a well overshadowed by palm trees under which they had previously concealed a store of provisions. Not surmising that the notion of flight would occur to their prisoner, they contented themselves with binding his hands, and after eating a few dates, and giving provender to their horses, went to sleep.

When the brave Provencal saw that his enemies were no longer watching him, he made use of his teeth to steal a scimiter, fixed the blade between his knees, and cut the cords which prevented him from using his hands; in a moment he was free. He at once seized a rifle and a dagger, then taking the precautions to provide himself with a sack of dried dates, oats, and powder and shot, and to fasten a scimiter to his waist, he leaped on to a horse, and spurred on vigorously in the direction where he thought to find the French army. So impatient was he to see a bivouac again that he pressed on the already tired courser at such speed, that its flanks were lacerated with his spurs, and at last the poor animal died, leaving the Frenchman alone in the desert. After walking some time in the sand with all the courage of an escaped convict, the soldier was obliged to stop, as the day had already ended. In spite of the beauty of an Oriental sky at night, he felt he had not strength enough to go on. Fortunately he had been able to find a small hill, on the summit of which a few palm trees shot up into the air; it was their verdure seen from afar which had brought hope and consolation to his heart. His fatigue was so great that he lay down upon a rock of granite, capriciously cut out like a camp-bed; there he fell asleep without taking any precaution to defend himself while he slept. He had made the sacrifice of his life. His last thought was one of regret. He repented having left the Maugrabins, whose nomadic life seemed to smile upon him now that he was far from them and without help. He was awakened by the sun, whose pitiless rays fell with all their force on the granite and produced an intolerable heat—for he had had the stupidity to place himself adversely to the shadow thrown by the verdant majestic heads of the palm trees. He looked at the solitary trees and shuddered—they reminded him of the graceful shafts crowned with foliage which characterize the Saracen columns in the cathedral of Arles.

But when, after counting the palm trees, he cast his eyes around him, the most horrible despair was infused into his soul. Before him stretched an ocean without limit. The dark sand of the desert spread further than eye could reach in every direction, and glittered like steel struck with bright light. It might have been a sea of looking-glass, or lakes melted together in a mirror. A fiery vapour carried up in surging waves made a perpetual whirlwind over the quivering land. The sky was lit with an Oriental splendour of insupportable purity, leaving naught for the imagination to desire. Heaven and earth were on fire.

The silence was awful in its wild and terrible majesty. Infinity, immensity, closed in upon the soul from every side. Not a cloud in the sky, not a breath in the air, not a flaw on the bosom of the sand, ever moving in diminutive waves; the horizon ended as at sea on a clear day, with one line of light, definite as the cut of a sword.

The Provencal threw his arms round the trunk of one of the palm trees, as though it were the body of a friend, and then, in the shelter of the thin, straight shadow that the palm cast upon the granite, he wept. Then sitting down he remained as he was, contemplating with profound sadness the implacable scene, which was all he had to look upon. He cried aloud, to measure the solitude. His voice, lost in the hollows of the hill, sounded faintly, and aroused no echo—the echo was in his own heart. The Provencal was twenty-two years old:—he loaded his carbine.

'There'll be time enough,' he said to himself, laying on the ground the weapon which alone could bring him deliverance.

Viewing alternately the dark expanse of the desert and the blue expanse of the sky, the soldier dreamed of France—he smelled with delight the gutters of Paris—he remembered the towns through which he had passed, the faces of his comrades, the most minute details of his life. His Southern fancy soon showed him the stones of his beloved Provence, in the play of the heat which undulated above the wide expanse of the desert. Realizing the danger of this cruel mirage, he went down the opposite side of the hill to that by which he had come up the day before. The remains of a rug showed that this place of refuge had at one time been inhabited; at a short distance he saw some palm trees full of dates. Then the instinct which binds us to life awoke again in his heart. He hoped to live long enough to await the passing of some Maugrabins, or perhaps he might hear the sound of cannon; for at this time Bonaparte was traversing Egypt.

This thought gave him new life. The palm tree seemed to bend with the weight of the ripe fruit. He shook some of it down. When he tasted this unhoped-for manna, he felt sure that the palms had been cultivated by a former inhabitant—the savoury, fresh meat of the dates were proof of the care of his predecessor. He passed suddenly from dark despair to an almost insane joy. He went up again to the top of the hill, and spent the rest of the day in cutting down one of the sterile palm trees, which the night before had served him for shelter. A vague memory made him think of the animals of the desert; and in case they might come to drink at the spring, visible from the base of the rocks but lost further down, he resolved to guard himself from their visits by placing a barrier at the entrance of his hermitage.

In spite of his diligence, and the strength which the fear of being devoured asleep gave him, he was unable to cut the palm in pieces, though he succeeded in cutting it down. At eventide the king of the desert fell; the sound of its fall resounded far and wide, like a sigh in the solitude; the soldier shuddered as though he had heard some voice predicting woe.

But like an heir who does not long bewail a deceased relative, he tore off from this beautiful tree the tall broad green leaves which are its poetic adornment, and used them to mend the mat on which he was to sleep.

Fatigued by the heat and his work, he fell asleep under the red curtains of his wet cave.

In the middle of the night his sleep was troubled by an extraordinary noise; he sat up, and the deep silence around allowed him to distinguish the alternative accents of a respiration whose savage energy could not belong to a human creature.

A profound terror, increased still further by the darkness, the silence, and his waking images, froze his heart within him. He almost felt his hair stand on end, when by straining his eyes to their utmost he perceived through the shadow two faint yellow lights. At first he attributed these lights to the reflections of his own pupils, but soon the vivid brilliance of the night aided him gradually to distinguish the objects around him in the cave, and he beheld a huge animal lying but two steps from him. Was it a lion, a tiger, or a crocodile?

The Provencal was not sufficiently educated to know under what species his enemy ought to be classed; but his fright was all the greater, as his ignorance led him to imagine all terrors at once; he endured a cruel torture, noting every variation of the breathing close to him without daring to make the slightest movement. An odour, pungent like that of a fox, but more penetrating, more profound,—so to speak,—filled the cave, and when the Provencal became sensible of this, his terror reached its height, for he could no longer doubt the proximity of a terrible companion, whose royal dwelling served him for a shelter.

Presently the reflection of the moon descending on the horizon lit up the den, rendering gradually visible and resplendent the spotted skin of a panther.

This lion of Egypt slept, curled up like a big dog, the peaceful possessor of a sumptuous niche at the gate of an hotel; its eyes opened for a moment and closed again; its face was turned towards the man. A thousand confused thoughts passed through the Frenchman's mind; first he thought of killing it with a bullet from his gun, but he saw there was not enough distance between them for him to take proper aim—the shot would miss the mark. And if it were to wake!—the thought made his limbs rigid. He listened to his own heart beating in the midst of the silence, and cursed the too violent pulsations which the flow of blood brought on, fearing to disturb that sleep which allowed him time to think of some means of escape.

Twice he placed his hand on his scimitar, intending to cut off the head of his enemy; but the difficulty of cutting the stiff short hair compelled him to abandon this daring project. To miss would be to die for certain, he thought; he preferred the chances of fair fight, and made up his mind to wait till morning; the morning did not leave him long to wait.

He could now examine the panther at ease; its muzzle was smeared with blood.

'She's had a good dinner,' he thought, without troubling himself as to whether her feast might have been on human flesh. 'She won't be hungry when she gets up.'

It was a female. The fur on her belly and flanks was glistening white; many small marks like velvet formed beautiful bracelets round her feet; her sinuous tail was also white, ending with black rings; the overpart of her dress, yellow like burnished gold, very lissom and soft, had the characteristic blotches in the form of rosettes, which distinguish the panther from every other feline species.

This tranquil and formidable hostess snored in an attitude as graceful as that of a cat lying on a cushion. Her blood-stained paws, nervous and well armed, were stretched out before her face, which rested upon them, and from which radiated her straight slender whiskers, like threads of silver.

If she had been like that in a cage, the Provencal would doubtless have admired the grace of the animal, and the vigorous contrasts of vivid colour which gave her robe an imperial splendour; but just then his sight was troubled by her sinister appearance.

The presence of the panther, even asleep, could not fail to produce the effect which the magnetic eyes of the serpent are said to have on the nightingale.

For a moment the courage of the soldier began to fail before this danger, though no doubt it would have risen at the mouth of a cannon charged with shell. Nevertheless, a bold thought brought daylight to his soul and sealed up the source of the cold sweat which sprang forth on his brow. Like men driven to bay, who defy death and offer their body to the smiter, so he, seeing in this merely a tragic episode, resolved to play his part with honour to the last.

'The day before yesterday the Arabs would have killed me, perhaps,' he said; so considering himself as good as dead already, he waited bravely, with excited curiosity, the awakening of his enemy.

When the sun appeared, the panther suddenly opened her eyes; then she put out her paws with energy, as if to stretch them and get rid of cramp. At last she yawned, showing the formidable apparatus of her teeth and pointed tongue, rough as a file.

'A regular petite maitresse,' thought the Frenchman, seeing her roll herself about so softly and coquettishly. She licked off the blood which stained her paws and muzzle, and scratched her head with reiterated gestures full of prettiness. 'All right, make a little toilet,' the Frenchman said to himself, beginning to recover his gaiety with his courage; 'we'll say good morning to each other presently;' and he seized the small, short dagger which he had taken from the Maugrabins.

At this moment the panther turned her head toward the man and looked at him fixedly without moving. The rigidity of her metallic eyes and their insupportable lustre made him shudder, especially when the animal walked towards him. But he looked at her caressingly, staring into her eyes in order to magnetize her, and let her come quite close to him; then with a movement both gentle and amorous, as though he were caressing the most beautiful of women, he passed his hand over her whole body, from the head to the tail, scratching the flexible vertebrae which divided the panther's yellow back. The animal waved her tail voluptuously, and her eyes grew gentle; and when for the third time the Frenchman accomplished this interesting flattery, she gave forth one of those purrings by which cats express their pleasure; but this murmur issued from a throat so powerful and so deep that it resounded through the cave like the last vibrations of an organ in a church. The man, understanding the importance of his caresses, redoubled them in such a way as to surprise and stupefy his imperious courtesan. When he felt sure of having extinguished the ferocity of his capricious companion, whose hunger had so fortunately been satisfied the day before, he got up to go out of the cave; the panther let him go out, but when he had reached the summit of the hill she sprang with the lightness of a sparrow hopping from twig to twig, and rubbed herself against his legs, putting up her back after the manner of all the race of cats. Then regarding her guest with eyes whose glare had softened a little, she gave vent to that wild cry which naturalists compare to the grating of a saw.

'She is exacting,' said the Frenchman, smilingly.

He was bold enough to play with her ears; he caressed her belly and scratched her head as hard as he could. When he saw that he was successful, he tickled her skull with the point of his dagger, watching for the right moment to kill her, but the hardness of her bones made him tremble for his success.

The sultana of the desert showed herself gracious to her slave; she lifted her head, stretched out her neck and manifested her delight by the tranquillity of her attitude. It suddenly occurred to the soldier that to kill this savage princess with one blow he must poniard her in the throat.

He raised the blade, when the panther, satisfied no doubt, laid herself gracefully at his feet, and cast up at him glances in which, in spite of their natural fierceness, was mingled confusedly a kind of good will. The poor Provencal ate his dates, leaning against one of the palm trees, and casting his eyes alternately on the desert in quest of some liberator and on his terrible companion to watch her uncertain clemency.

The panther looked at the place where the date stones fell, and every time that he threw one down her eyes expressed an incredible mistrust.

She examined the man with an almost commercial prudence. However, this examination was favourable to him, for when he had finished his meagre meal she licked his boots with her powerful rough tongue, brushing off with marvellous skill the dust gathered in the creases.

'Ah, but when she's really hungry!' thought the Frenchman. In spite of the shudder this thought caused him, the soldier began to measure curiously the proportions of the panther, certainly one of the most splendid specimens of its race. She was three feet high and four feet long without counting her tail; this powerful weapon, rounded like a cudgel, was nearly three feet long. The head, large as that of a lioness, was distinguished by a rare expression of refinement. The cold cruelty of a tiger was dominant, it was true, but there was also a vague resemblance to the face of a sensual woman. Indeed, the face of this solitary queen had something of the gaiety of a drunken Nero: she had satiated herself with blood, and she wanted to play.

The soldier tried if he might walk up and down, and the panther left him free, contenting herself with following him with her eyes, less like a faithful dog than a big Angora cat, observing everything and every movement of her master.

When he looked around, he saw, by the spring, the remains of his horse; the panther had dragged the carcass all that way; about two thirds of it had been devoured already. The sight reassured him.

It was easy to explain the panther's absence, and the respect she had had for him while he slept. The first piece of good luck emboldened him to tempt the future, and he conceived the wild hope of continuing on good terms with the panther during the entire day, neglecting no means of taming her, and remaining in her good graces.

He returned to her, and had the unspeakable joy of seeing her wag her tail with an almost imperceptible movement at his approach. He sat down then, without fear, by her side, and they began to play together; he took her paws and muzzle, pulled her ears, rolled her over on her back, stroked her warm, delicate flanks. She let him do whatever he liked, and when he began to stroke the hair on her feet she drew her claws in carefully.

The man, keeping the dagger in one hand, thought to plunge it into the belly of the too confiding panther, but he was afraid that he would be immediately strangled in her last convulsive struggle; besides, he felt in his heart a sort of remorse which bid him respect a creature that had done him no harm. He seemed to have found a friend, in a boundless desert; half unconsciously he thought of his first sweetheart, whom he had nicknamed 'Mignonne' by way of contrast, because she was so atrociously jealous that all the time of their love he was in fear of the knife with which she had always threatened him.

This memory of his early days suggested to him the idea of making the young panther answer to this name, now that he began to admire with less terror her swiftness, suppleness, and softness. Toward the end of the day he had familiarized himself with his perilous position; he now almost liked the painfulness of it. At last his companion had got into the habit of looking up at him whenever he cried in a falsetto voice, 'Mignonne'.

At the setting of the sun Mignonne gave, several times running, a profound melancholy cry. 'She's been well brought up,' said the light-hearted soldier, 'she says her prayers.' But this mental joke only occurred to him when he noticed what a pacific attitude his companion remained in. 'Come, ma petite blonde, I'll let you go to bed first,' he said to her, counting on the activity of his own legs to run away as quickly as possible, directly she was asleep, and seek another shelter for the night.

The soldier waited with impatience the hour of his flight, and when it had arrived he walked vigorously in the direction of the Nile; but hardly had he made a quarter of a league in the sand when he heard the panther bounding after him, crying with that saw-like cry more dreadful even than the sound of her leaping.

'Ah!' he said, 'then she's taken a fancy to me, she has never met anyone before, and it is really quite flattering to have her first love.' That instant the man fell into one of those movable quicksands so terrible to travellers and from which it is impossible to save oneself. Feeling himself caught, he gave a shriek of alarm; the panther seized him with her teeth by the collar, and, springing vigorously backwards, drew him as if by magic out of the whirling sand.

'Ah, Mignonne!' cried the soldier, caressing her enthusiastically; 'we're bound together for life and death but no jokes, mind!' and he retraced his steps.

From that time the desert seemed inhabited. It contained a being to whom the man could talk, and whose ferocity was rendered gentle by him, though he could not explain to himself the reason for their strange friendship. Great as was the soldier's desire to stay upon guard, he slept.

On awakening he could not find Mignonne; he mounted the hill, and in the distance saw her springing toward him after the habit of these animals, who cannot run on account of the extreme flexibility of the vertebral column. Mignonne arrived, her jaws covered with blood; she received the wonted caress of her companion, showing with much purring how happy it made her. Her eyes, full of languor, turned still more gently than the day before toward the Provencal, who talked to her as one would to a tame animal.

'Ah! Mademoiselle, you are a nice girl, aren't you? Just look at that! So we like to be made much of, don't we? Aren't you ashamed of yourself? So you have been eating some Arab or other, have you? That doesn't matter. They're animals just the same as you are; but don't you take to eating Frenchmen, or I shan't like you any longer.'

She played like a dog with its master, letting herself be rolled over, knocked about, and stroked, alternately; sometimes she herself would provoke the soldier, putting up her paw with a soliciting gesture.

Some days passed in this manner. This companionship permitted the Provencal to appreciate the sublime beauty of the desert; now that he had a living thing to think about, alternations of fear and quiet, and plenty to eat, his mind became filled with contrast and his life began to be diversified.

Solitude revealed to him all her secrets, and enveloped him in her delights. He discovered in the rising and setting of the sun sights unknown to the world. He knew what it was to tremble when he heard over his head the hiss of a bird's wing, so rarely did they pass, or when he saw the clouds, changing and many coloured travellers, melt one into another. He studied in the night time the effect of the moon upon the ocean of sand, where the simoom made waves swift of movement and rapid in their change. He lived the life of the Eastern day, marvelling at its wonderful pomp; then, after having revelled in the sight of a hurricane over the plain where the whirling sands made red, dry mists and death-bearing clouds, he would welcome the night with joy, for then fell the healthful freshness of the stars, and he listened to imaginary music in the skies. Then solitude taught him to unroll the treasures of dreams. He passed whole hours in remembering mere nothings, and comparing his present life with his past.

At last he grew passionately fond of the panther; for some

sort of affection was a necessity.

Whether it was that his will powerfully projected had modified the character of his companion, or whether, because she found abundant food in her predatory excursions in the desert, she respected the man's life, he began to fear for it no longer, seeing her so well tamed.

He devoted the greater part of his time to sleep, but he was obliged to watch like a spider in its web that the moment of his deliverance might not escape him, if anyone should pass the line marked by the horizon. He had sacrificed his shirt to make a flag with, which he hung at the top of a palm tree, whose foliage he had torn off. Taught by necessity, he found the means of keeping it spread out, by fastening it with little sticks; for the wind might not be blowing at the moment when the passing traveller was looking through the desert.

It was during the long hours, when he had abandoned hope, that he amused himself with the panther. He had come to learn the different inflections of her voice, the expressions of her eyes; he had studied the capricious patterns of all the rosettes which marked the gold of her robe. Mignonne was not even angry when he took hold of the tuft at the end of her tail to count her rings, those graceful ornaments which glittered in the sun like jewelry. It gave him pleasure to contemplate the supple, fine outlines of her form, the whiteness of her belly, the graceful pose of her head. But it was especially when she was playing that he felt most pleasure in looking at her; the agility and youthful lightness of her movements were a continual surprise to him; he wondered at the supple way in which she jumped and climbed, washed herself and arranged her fur, crouched down and prepared to spring. However rapid her spring might be, however slippery the stone she was on, she would always stop short at the word 'Mignonne'.

One day, in a bright midday sun, an enormous bird coursed through the air. The man left his panther to look at his new guest;

but after waiting a moment the deserted sultana growled deeply.

'My goodness! I do believe she's jealous,' he cried, seeing her eyes become hard again; 'the soul of Virginie has passed into her body; that's certain.'

The eagle disappeared into the air, while the soldier admired the curved contour of the panther.

But there was such youth and grace in her form! She was beautiful as a woman! The blond fur of her robe mingled well with the delicate tints of faint white which marked her flanks.

The profuse light cast down by the sun made this living gold, these russet markings, to burn in a way to give them an indefinable attraction.

The man and the panther looked at one another with a look full of meaning; the coquette quivered when she felt her friend stroke her head; her eyes flashed like lightning—then she shut them tightly.

'She has a soul,' he said, looking at the stillness of this queen of the sands, golden like them, white like them, solitary and burning like them.

'Well,' she said, 'I have read your plea in favour of beasts; but how did two so well adapted to understand each other end?'

'Ah, well! You see, they ended as all great passions do end— by a misunderstanding. For some reason one suspects the other of treason; they don't come to an explanation through pride, and quarrel and part from sheer obstinacy.'

'Yet sometimes at the best moments a single word or a look is enough—but anyhow go on with your story.'

'It's horribly difficult, but you will understand, after what the old villain told me over his champagne. He said—"I don't know if I hurt her, but she turned round, as if enraged, and with her sharp teeth caught hold of my leg—gently, I daresay; but I, thinking she would devour me, plunged my dagger into her throat. She rolled over, giving a cry that froze my heart; and I saw her dying, still looking at me without anger. I would have given all the world—my cross even, which I had not got then—to have brought her to life again. It was as though I had murdered a real person; and the soldiers who had seen my flag, and were come to my assistance, found me in tears."

"'Well sir," he said, after a moment of silence, "since then I have been in war in Germany, in Spain, in Russia, in France; I've certainly carried my carcase about a good deal, but never have I seen anything like the desert. Ah! Yes, it is very beautiful!'"

"'What did you feel there?' I asked him.

"'Oh! That can't be described, young man! Besides, I am not always regretting my palm trees and my panther. I should have to be very melancholy for that. In the desert, you see, there is everything and nothing.'"

"'Yes, but explain—'"

"'Well,' he said, with an impatient gesture, 'it is God without mankind.'"

5

THE MESSAGE

I have always longed to tell a simple and true story, which should strike terror into two young lovers, and drive them to take refuge each in the other's heart, as two children cling together at the sight of a snake by a woodside. At the risk of spoiling my story and of being taken for a coxcomb, I state my intention at the outset.

I myself played a part in this almost commonplace tragedy; so if it fails to interest you, the failure will be in part my own fault, in part owing to historical veracity. Plenty of things in real life are superlatively uninteresting; so that it is one-half of art to select from realities those which contain possibilities of poetry.

In 1819 I was travelling from Paris to Moulins. The state of my finances obliged me to take an outside place. Englishmen, as you know, regard those airy perches on the top of the coach as the best seats; and for the first few miles I discovered abundance of excellent reasons for justifying the opinion of our neighbours. A young fellow, apparently in somewhat better circumstances, who came to take the seat beside me from preference, listened to my reasoning with inoffensive smiles. An approximate nearness of age, a similarity in ways of thinking, a common love of fresh air, and of the rich landscape scenery through which the coach was lumbering along,—these things, together with an indescribable magnetic something, drew us before long into one of those short-lived traveller's intimacies, in which we unbend with the more complacency because the intercourse is by its very nature transient, and makes no implicit demands upon the future.

We had not come thirty leagues before we were talking of women and love. Then, with all the circumspection demanded in such matters, we proceeded naturally to the topic of our lady-loves. Young as we both were, we still admired 'the woman of a certain age', that is to say, the woman between thirty-five and forty. Oh! Any poet who should have listened to our talk, for heaven knows how many stages beyond Montargis, would have reaped a harvest of flaming epithet, rapturous description, and very tender confidences. Our bashful fears, our silent interjections, our blushes, as we met each other's eyes, were expressive with an eloquence, a boyish charm, which I have ceased to feel. One must remain young, no doubt, to understand youth.

Well, we understood one another to admiration on all the essential points of passion. We had laid it down as an axiom at the very outset, that in theory and practice there was no such piece of drivelling nonsense in this world as a certificate of birth; that plenty of women were younger at forty than many a girl of twenty; and, to come to the point, that a woman is no older than she looks.

This theory set no limits to the age of love, so we struck out, in all good faith, into a boundless sea. At length, when we had portrayed our mistresses as young, charming, and devoted to us, women of rank, women of taste, intellectual and clever; when we had endowed them with little feet, a satin, nay, a delicately fragrant skin, then came the admission—on his part that Madame Such-an-one was thirty-eight years old, and on mine that I worshipped a woman of forty. Whereupon, as if released on either side from some kind of vague fear, our confidences came thick and fast, when we found that we were in the same confraternity of love. It was which of us should overtop the other in sentiment.

One of us had travelled six hundred miles to see his mistress for an hour. The other, at the risk of being shot for a wolf, had prowled about her park to meet her one night. Out came all our follies in fact. If it is pleasant to remember past dangers, is it not at least as pleasant to recall past delights? We live through the joy a second time. We told each other everything, our perils, our great joys, our little pleasures, and even the humours of the situation. My friend's countess had lighted a cigar for him; mine made chocolate for me, and wrote to me every day when we did not meet; his lady had come to spend three days with him at the risk of ruin to her reputation; mine had done even better, or worse, if you will have it so. Our countesses, moreover, were adored by their husbands; these gentlemen were enslaved by the charm possessed by every woman who loves; and, with even supererogatory simplicity, afforded us that just sufficient spice of danger which increases pleasure. Ah! How quickly the wind swept away our talk and our happy laughter!

When we reached Pouilly, I scanned my new friend with much interest, and truly, it was not difficult to imagine him the hero of a very serious love affair. Picture to yourselves a young man of middle height, but very well proportioned, a bright, expressive face, dark hair, blue eyes, moist lips, and white and even teeth. A certain not unbecoming pallor still overspread his delicately cut features, and there were faint dark circles about his eyes, as if he were recovering from an illness. Add, furthermore, that he had white and shapely hands, of which he was as careful as a pretty woman should be; add that he seemed to be very well informed, and was decidedly clever, and it should not be difficult for you to imagine that my travelling companion was more than worthy of a countess. Indeed, many a girl might have wished for such a husband, for he was a Vicomte with an income of twelve or fifteen thousand livres, 'to say nothing of expectations'.

About a league out of Pouilly the coach was overturned. My

luckless comrade, thinking to save himself, jumped to the edge of a newly-ploughed field, instead of following the fortunes of the vehicle and clinging tightly to the roof, as I did. He either miscalculated in some way, or he slipped; how it happened, I do not know, but the coach fell over upon him, and he was crushed under it.

We carried him into a peasant's cottage, and there, amid the moans wrung from him by horrible sufferings, he contrived to give me a commission—a sacred task, in that it was laid upon me by a dying man's last wish. Poor boy, all through his agony he was torturing himself in his young simplicity of heart with the thought of the painful shock to his mistress when she should suddenly read of his death in a newspaper. He begged me to go myself to break the news to her. He bade me look for a key which he wore on a ribbon about his neck. I found it half buried in the flesh, but the dying boy did not utter a sound as I extricated it as gently as possible from the wound which it had made. He had scarcely given me the necessary directions—I was to go to his home at La Charite-sur-Loire for his mistress' love-letters, which he conjured me to return to her—when he grew speechless in the middle of a sentence; but from his last gesture, I understood that the fatal key would be my passport in his mother's house. It troubled him that he was powerless to utter a single word to thank me, for of my wish to serve him he had no doubt. He looked wistfully at me for a moment, then his eyelids drooped in token of farewell, and his head sank, and he died. His death was the only fatal accident caused by the overturn.

'But it was partly his own fault,' the coachman said to me.

At La Charite, I executed the poor fellow's dying wishes. His mother was away from home, which in a manner was fortunate for me. Nevertheless, I had to assuage the grief of an old woman-servant, who staggered back at the tidings of her young master's death, and sank half-dead into a chair when she saw the blood-stained key. But I had another and more dreadful sorrow to think of, the sorrow of a woman who had lost her last love; so I left the old woman to her prosopopeia, and carried off the precious correspondence, carefully sealed by my friend of the day.

The Countess' chateau was some eight leagues beyond Moulins, and then there was some distance to walk across country. So it was not exactly an easy matter to deliver my message. For diverse reasons into which I need not enter, I had barely sufficient money to take me to Moulins. However, my youthful enthusiasm determined to hasten thither on foot as fast as possible. Bad news travels swiftly, and I wished to be first at the chateau. I asked for the shortest way, and hurried through the field paths of the Bourbonnais, bearing, as it were, a dead man on my back. The nearer I came to the Chateau de Montpersan, the more aghast I felt at the idea of my strange self-imposed pilgrimage. Vast numbers of romantic fancies ran in my head. I imagined all kinds of situations in which I might find this Comtesse de Montpersan, or, to observe the laws of romance, this Juliette, so passionately beloved of my travelling companion. I sketched out ingenious answers to the questions which she might be supposed to put to me. At every turn of a wood, in every beaten pathway, I rehearsed a modern version of the scene in which Sosie describes the battle to his lantern. To my shame be it said, I had thought at first of nothing but the part that I was to play, of my own cleverness, of how I should demean myself; but now that I was in the country, an ominous thought flashed through my soul like a thunderbolt tearing its way through a veil of gray cloud.

What an awful piece of news it was for a woman whose whole thoughts were full of her young lover, who was looking forward hour by hour to a joy which no words can express, a woman who had been at a world of pains to invent plausible pretexts to draw him to her side. Yet, after all, it was a cruel deed of charity to be the messenger of death! So I hurried on, splashing and bemiring myself in the byways of the Bourbonnais.

Before very long I reached a great chestnut avenue with a pile of buildings at the further end—the Chateau of Montpersan stood out against the sky like a mass of brown cloud, with sharp, fantastic outlines. All the doors of the chateau stood open. This in itself disconcerted me, and routed all my plans; but I went in boldly, and in a moment found myself between a couple of dogs, barking as your true country-bred animal can bark. The sound brought out a hurrying servant-maid, who, when informed that I wished to speak to Mme. la Comtesse, waved a hand towards the masses of trees in the English park which wound about the chateau with 'Madame is out there—'

'Many thanks,' said I ironically. I might have wandered for a couple of hours in the park with her 'out there' to guide me.

In the meantime, a pretty little girl, with curling hair, dressed in a white frock, a rose-coloured sash, and a broad frill at the throat, had overheard or guessed the question and its answer. She gave me a glance and vanished, calling in shrill, childish tones:

'Mother, here is a gentleman who wishes to speak to you!'

And, along the winding alleys, I followed the skipping and dancing white frill, a sort of will-o'-the-wisp, that showed me the way among the trees.

I must make a full confession. I stopped behind the last shrub in the avenue, pulled up my collar, rubbed my shabby hat and my trousers with the cuffs of my sleeves, dusted my coat with the sleeves themselves, and gave them a final cleansing rub one against the other. I buttoned my coat carefully so as to exhibit the inner, always the least worn, side of the cloth, and finally had turned down the tops of my trousers over my boots, artistically cleaned in the grass. Thanks to this Gascon toilet, I could hope that the lady would not take me for the local rate collector; but now when my thoughts travel back to that episode of my youth, I sometimes laugh at my own expense.

Suddenly, just as I was composing myself, at a turning in the green walk, among a wilderness of flowers lighted up by a hot ray of sunlight, I saw Juliette—Juliette and her husband. The pretty little girl held her mother by the hand, and it was easy to see that the lady had quickened her pace somewhat at the child's ambiguous phrase. Taken aback by the sight of a total stranger, who bowed with a tolerably awkward air, she looked at me with a coolly courteous expression and an adorable pout, in which I, who knew her secret, could read the full extent of her disappointment. I sought, but sought in vain, to remember any of the elegant phrases so laboriously prepared.

This momentary hesitation gave the lady's husband time to come forward. Thoughts by the myriad flitted through my brain. To give myself a countenance, I got out a few sufficiently feeble inquiries, asking whether the persons present were really M. le Comte and Mme. la Comtesse de Montpersan. These imbecilities gave me time to form my own conclusions at a glance, and, with a perspicacity rare at that age, to analyze the husband and wife whose solitude was about to be so rudely disturbed.

The husband seemed to be a specimen of a certain type of nobleman, the fairest ornaments of the provinces of our day. He wore big shoes with stout soles to them. I put the shoes first advisedly, for they made an even deeper impression upon me than a seedy black coat, a pair of threadbare trousers, a flabby cravat, or a crumpled shirt collar. There was a touch of the magistrate in the man, a good deal more of the Councillor of the Prefecture, all the self-importance of the mayor of the arrondissement, the local autocrat, and the soured temper of the unsuccessful candidate who has never been returned since the year 1816. As to countenance—a wizened, wrinkled, sunburned face, and long, sleek locks of scanty gray hair; as to character—an incredible mixture of homely sense and sheer silliness; of a rich man's overbearing ways, and a total lack of manners; just the kind of husband who is almost entirely led by his wife, yet imagines himself to be the master; apt to domineer in trifles, and to let more important things slip past unheeded—there you have the man!

But the Countess! Ah, how sharp and startling the contrast between husband and wife! The Countess was a little woman, with a flat, graceful figure and enchanting shape; so fragile, so dainty was she, that you would have feared to break some bone if you so much as touched her. She wore a white muslin dress, a rose-coloured sash, and rose-coloured ribbons in the pretty cap on her head; her chemisette was moulded so deliciously by her shoulders and the loveliest rounded contours, that the sight of her awakened an irresistible desire of possession in the depths of the heart. Her eyes were bright and dark and expressive, her movements graceful, her foot charming. An experienced man of pleasure would not have given her more than thirty years, her forehead was so girlish. She had all the most transient delicate detail of youth in her face. In character she seemed to me to resemble the Comtesse de Lignolles and the Marquise de B—, two feminine types always fresh in the memory of any young man who has read Louvet's romance.

In a moment I saw how things stood, and took a diplomatic course that would have done credit to an old ambassador. For once, and perhaps for the only time in my life, I used tact, and knew in what the special skill of courtiers and men of the world consists.

I have had so many battles to fight since those heedless days, that they have left me no time to distil all the least actions of daily life, and to do everything so that it falls in with those rules of etiquette and good taste which wither the most generous emotions.

'M. le Comte,' I said with an air of mystery, 'I should like a few words with you,' and I fell back a pace or two.

He followed my example. Juliette left us together, going away unconcernedly, like a wife who knew that she can learn her husband's secrets as soon as she chooses to know them.

I told the Count briefly of the death of my travelling companion. The effect produced by my news convinced me that his affection for his young collaborator was cordial enough, and this emboldened me to make reply as I did.

'My wife will be in despair,' cried he; 'I shall be obliged to break the news of this unhappy event with great caution.'

'Monsieur,' said I, 'I addressed myself to you in the first instance, as in duty bound. I could not, without first informing you, deliver a message to Mme. la Comtesse, a message intrusted to me by an entire stranger; but this commission is a sort of sacred trust, a secret of which I have no power to dispose. From the high idea of your character which he gave me, I felt sure that you would not oppose me in the fulfilment of a dying request. Mme. la Comtesse will be at liberty to break the silence which is imposed upon me.'

At this eulogy, the Count swung his head very amiably, responded with a tolerably involved compliment, and finally left me a free field. We returned to the house. The bell rang, and I was invited to dinner. As we came up to the house, a grave and silent couple, Juliette stole a glance at us. Not a little surprised to find her husband contriving some frivolous excuse for leaving us together, she stopped short, giving me a glance—such a glance as women only can give you. In that look of hers there was the pardonable curiosity of the mistress of the house confronted with a guest dropped down upon her from the skies and innumerable doubts, certainly warranted by the state of my clothes, by my youth and my expression, all singularly at variance; there was all the disdain of the adored mistress, in whose eyes all men save one are as nothing; there were involuntary tremors and alarms; and, above all, the thought that it was tiresome to have an unexpected guest just now, when, no doubt, she had been scheming to enjoy full solitude for her love. This mute eloquence I understood in her eyes, and all the pity and compassion in me made answer in a sad smile. I thought of her, as I had seen her for one moment, in the pride of her beauty; standing in the sunny afternoon in the narrow alley with the flowers on either hand; and as that fair wonderful picture rose before my eyes, I could not repress a sigh.

'Alas, madame, I have just made a very arduous journey—, undertaken solely on your account.'

'Sir!'

'Oh! It is on behalf of one who calls you Juliette that I am come,' I continued. Her face grew white.

'You will not see him today.'

'Is he ill?' she asked, and her voice sank lower.

'Yes. But for pity's sake, control yourself... He intrusted me with secrets that concern you, and you may be sure that never messenger could be more discreet nor more devoted than I.'

'What is the matter with him?'

'How if he loved you no longer?'

'Oh! That is impossible!' she cried, and a faint smile, nothing less than frank, broke over her face. Then all at once a kind of shudder ran through her, and she reddened, and she gave me a wild, swift glance as she asked:

'Is he alive?'

Great God! What a terrible phrase! I was too young to bear that tone in her voice; I made no reply, only looked at the unhappy woman in helpless bewilderment.

'Monsieur, monsieur, give me an answer!' she cried.

'Yes, madame.'

'Is it true? Oh! Tell me the truth; I can hear the truth. Tell me the truth! Any pain would be less keen than this suspense.'

I answered by two tears wrung from me by that strange tone of hers. She leaned against a tree with a faint, sharp cry.

'Madame, here comes your husband!'

'Have I a husband?' and with those words she fled away out of sight.

'Well,' cried the Count, 'dinner is growing cold.—Come, monsieur.'

Thereupon I followed the master of the house into the dining-room. Dinner was served with all the luxury which we have learned to expect in Paris. There were five covers laid, three for the Count and Countess and their little daughter; my own, which should have been his; and another for the canon of Saint-Denis, who said grace, and then asked:

'Why, where can our dear Countess be?'

'Oh! she will be here directly,' said the Count. He had hastily helped us to the soup, and was dispatching an ample plateful with portentous speed.

'Oh! Nephew,' exclaimed the canon, 'if your wife were here, you would behave more rationally.'

'Papa will make himself ill!' said the child with a mischievous look.

Just after this extraordinary gastronomical episode, as the Count was eagerly helping himself to a slice of venison, a housemaid came in with, 'We cannot find Madame anywhere, sir!'

I sprang up at the words with a dread in my mind, my fears written so plainly in my face, that the old canon came out after me into the garden. The Count, for the sake of appearances, came as far as the threshold.

'Don't go, don't go!' called he. 'Don't trouble yourselves in the least,' but he did not offer to accompany us.

We three—the canon, the housemaid, and I—hurried through the garden walks and over the bowling-green in the park, shouting, listening for an answer, growing more uneasy every moment. As we hurried along, I told the story of the fatal accident, and discovered how strongly the maid was attached to her mistress, for she took my secret dread far more seriously than the canon. We went along by the pools of water; all over the park we went; but we neither found the Countess nor any sign that she had passed that way. At last we turned back, and under the walls of some outbuildings I heard a smothered, wailing cry, so stifled that it was scarcely audible. The sound seemed to come from a place that might have been a granary. I went in at all risks, and there we found Juliette. With the instinct of despair, she had buried herself deep in the hay, hiding her face in it to deaden those dreadful cries—prudency even stronger than grief. She was sobbing and crying like a child, but there was a more poignant, more piteous sound in the sobs. There was nothing left in the world for her. The maid pulled the hay from her, her mistress submitting with the supine listlessness of a dying animal. The maid could find nothing to say but 'There! Madame; there, there—'

'What is the matter with her? What is it, niece?' the old canon kept on exclaiming.

At last, with the girl's help, I carried Juliette to her room, gave orders that she was not to be disturbed, and that every one must be told that the Countess was suffering from a sick headache. Then we came down to the dining-room, the canon and I.

Some little time had passed since we left the dinner-table; I had scarcely given a thought to the Count since we left him under the peristyle; his indifference had surprised me, but my amazement increased when we came back and found him seated philosophically at table. He had eaten pretty nearly all the dinner, to the huge delight of his little daughter; the child was smiling at her father's flagrant infraction of the Countess' rules. The man's odd indifference was explained to me by a mild altercation which at once arose with the canon. The Count was suffering from some serious complaint. I cannot remember now what it was, but his medical advisers had put him on a very severe regimen, and the ferocious hunger familiar to convalescents, sheer animal appetite, had overpowered all human sensibilities. In that little space I had seen frank and undisguised human nature under two very different aspects, in such a sort that there was a certain grotesque element in the very midst of a most terrible tragedy.

The evening that followed was dreary. I was tired. The canon racked his brains to discover a reason for his niece's tears. The lady's husband silently digested his dinner; content, apparently, with the Countess' rather vague explanation, sent through the maid, putting forward some feminine ailment as her excuse. We all went early to bed.

As I passed the door of the Countess' room on the way to my night's lodging, I asked the servant timidly for news of her. She heard my voice, and would have me come in, and tried to talk, but in vain—she could not utter a sound. She bent her head, and I withdrew. In spite of the painful agitation, which I had felt to the full as youth can feel, I fell asleep, tired out with my forced march.

It was late in the night when I was awakened by the grating sound of curtain rings drawn sharply over the metal rods. There sat the Countess at the foot of my bed. The light from a lamp set on my table fell full upon her face.

'Is it really true, monsieur, quite true?' she asked. 'I do not know how I can live after that awful blow which struck me down a little while since; but just now I feel calm. I want to know everything.'

'What calm!' I said to myself as I saw the ghastly pallor of her face contrasting with her brown hair, and heard the guttural tones of her voice. The havoc wrought in her drawn features filled me with dumb amazement.

Those few hours had bleached her; she had lost a woman's last glow of autumn colour. Her eyes were red and swollen, nothing of their beauty remained, nothing looked out of them save her bitter and exceeding grief; it was as if a gray cloud covered the place through which the sun had shone.

I gave her the story of the accident in a few words, without laying too much stress on some too harrowing details. I told her about our first day's journey, and how it had been filled with recollections of her and of love. And she listened eagerly, without shedding a tear, leaning her face towards me, as some zealous doctor might lean to watch any change in a patient's face. When she seemed to me to have opened her whole heart to pain, to be deliberately plunging herself into misery with the first delirious frenzy of despair, I caught at my opportunity, and told her of the fears that troubled the poor dying man, told her how and why it was that he had given me this fatal message. Then her tears were dried by the fires that burned in the dark depths within her. She grew even paler. When I drew the letters from beneath my pillow and held them out to her, she took them mechanically; then, trembling from head to foot, she said in a hollow voice:

'And I burned all his letters!—I have nothing of him left!—Nothing! nothing!'

She struck her hand against her forehead.

'Madame—' I began.

She glanced at me in the convulsion of grief.

'I cut this from his head, this lock of his hair.'

And I gave her that last imperishable token that had been a very part of him she loved. Ah! If you had felt, as I felt then, her burning tears falling on your hands, you would know what gratitude is, when it follows so closely upon the benefit. Her eyes shone with a feverish glitter, a faint ray of happiness gleamed out of her terrible suffering, as she grasped my hands in hers, and said, in a choking voice:

'Ah! You love! May you be happy always. May you never lose her whom you love.'

She broke off, and fled away with her treasure.

Next morning, this night-scene among my dreams seemed like a dream; to make sure of the piteous truth, I was obliged to look fruitlessly under my pillow for the packet of letters. There is no need to tell you how the next day went. I spent several hours of it with the Juliette whom my poor comrade had so praised to me. In her lightest words, her gestures, in all that she did and said, I saw proofs of the nobleness of soul, the delicacy of feeling which made her what she was, one of those beloved, loving, and self-sacrificing natures so rarely found upon this earth.

In the evening the Comte de Montpersan came himself as far as Moulins with me. There he spoke with a kind of embarrassment:

'Monsieur, if it is not abusing your good nature, and acting very inconsiderately towards a stranger to whom we are already under obligations, would you have the goodness, as you are going to Paris, to remit a sum of money to M. de— (I forget the name), in the Rue du Sentier; I owe him an amount, and he asked me to send it as soon as possible.'

'Willingly,' said I. And in the innocence of my heart, I took charge of a rouleau of twenty-five louis d'or, which paid the expenses of my journey back to Paris; and only when, on my arrival, I went to the address indicated to repay the amount to M. de Montpersan's correspondent, did I understand the ingenious delicacy with which Juliette had obliged me. Was not all the genius of a loving woman revealed in such a way of lending, in her reticence with regard to a poverty easily guessed?

And what rapture to have this adventure to tell to a woman who clung to you more closely in dread, saying, 'Oh, my dear, not you! You must not die!'

6

THE RED INN

In I know not what year a Parisian banker, who had very extensive commercial relations with Germany, was entertaining at dinner one of those friends whom men of business often make in the markets of the world through correspondence; a man hitherto personally unknown to him. This friend, the head of a rather important house in Nuremburg, was a stout worthy German, a man of taste and erudition, above all a man of pipes, having a fine, broad, Nuremburgian face, with a square open forehead adorned by a few sparse locks of yellowish hair. He was the type of the sons of that pure and noble Germany, so fertile in honourable natures, whose peaceful manners and morals have never been lost, even after seven invasions.

This stranger laughed with simplicity, listened attentively, and drank remarkably well, seeming to like champagne as much perhaps as he liked his straw-coloured Johannisburger. His name was Hermann, which is that of most Germans whom authors bring upon their scene. Like a man who does nothing frivolously, he was sitting squarely at the banker's table and eating with that Teutonic appetite so celebrated throughout Europe, saying, in fact, a conscientious farewell to the cookery of the great Careme.

To do honour to his guest the master of the house had

invited a few intimate friends, capitalists or merchants, and several agreeable and pretty women, whose pleasant chatter and frank manners were in harmony with German cordiality. Really, if you could have seen, as I saw, this joyous gathering of persons who had drawn in their commercial claws, and were speculating only on the pleasures of life, you would have found no cause to hate usurious discounts, or to curse bankruptcies. Mankind can't always be doing evil. Even in the society of pirates one might find a few sweet hours during which we could fancy their sinister craft a pleasure-boat rocking on the deep.

'Before we part, Monsieur Hermann will, I trust, tell one more German story to terrify us?'

These words were said at dessert by a pale fair girl, who had read, no doubt, the tales of Hoffmann and the novels of Walter Scott. She was the only daughter of the banker, a charming young creature whose education was then being finished at the Gymnase, the plays of which she adored. At this moment the guests were in that happy state of laziness and silence which follows a delicious dinner, especially if we have presumed too far on our digestive powers. Leaning back in their chairs, their wrists lightly resting on the edge of the table, they were indolently playing with the gilded blades of their dessert-knives. When a dinner comes to this declining moment some guests will be seen to play with a pear seed; others roll crumbs of bread between their fingers and thumbs; lovers trace indistinct letters with fragments of fruit; misers count the stones on their plate and arrange them as a manager marshals his supernumeraries at the back of the stage. These are little gastronomic felicities which Brillat-Savarin, otherwise so complete an author, overlooked in his book. The footmen had disappeared. The dessert was like a squadron after a battle: all the dishes were disabled, pillaged, damaged; several were wandering around the table, in spite of the efforts of the mistress of the house to keep them in their places. Some of the persons present were gazing at pictures of Swiss scenery, symmetrically hung upon the gray-toned walls of the dining-room. Not a single guest was bored; in fact, I never yet knew a man who was sad during his digestion of a good dinner. We like at such moments to remain in quietude, a species of middle ground between the reverie of a thinker and the comfort of the ruminating animals; a condition which we may call the material melancholy of gastronomy.

So the guests now turned spontaneously to the excellent German, delighted to have a tale to listen to, even though it might prove of no interest. During this blessed interregnum the voice of a narrator is always delightful to our languid senses; it increases their negative happiness. I, a seeker after impressions, admired the faces about me, enlivened by smiles, beaming in the light of the wax candles, and somewhat flushed by our late good cheer; their diverse expressions producing piquant effects seen among the porcelain baskets, the fruits, the glasses, and the candelabra.

All of a sudden my imagination was caught by the aspect of a guest who sat directly in front of me. He was a man of medium height, rather fat and smiling, having the air and manner of a stock-broker, and apparently endowed with a very ordinary mind. Hitherto I had scarcely noticed him, but now his face, possibly darkened by a change in the lights, seemed to me to have altered its character; it had certainly grown ghastly; violet tones were spreading over it; you might have thought it the cadaverous head of a dying man. Motionless as the personages painted on a diorama, his stupefied eyes were fixed on the sparkling facets of a cut-glass stopper, but certainly without observing them; he seemed to be engulfed in some weird contemplation of the future or the past. When I had long examined that puzzling face I began to reflect about it. 'Is he ill?' I said to myself. 'Has he drunk too much wine? Is he ruined by a drop in the Funds? Is he thinking how to cheat his creditors?'

'Look!' I said to my neighbour, pointing out to her the face of the unknown man, 'is that an embryo bankrupt?'

'Oh, no!' she answered, 'he would be much gayer.' Then, nodding her head gracefully, she added, 'If that man ever ruins himself I'll tell it in Pekin! He possesses a million in real estate. That's a former purveyor to the imperial armies; a good sort of man, and rather original. He married a second time by way of speculation; but for all that he makes his wife extremely happy. He has a pretty daughter, whom he refused for many years to recognize; but the death of his son, unfortunately killed in a duel, has compelled him to take her home, for he could not otherwise have children. The poor girl has suddenly become one of the richest heiresses in Paris. The death of his son threw the poor man into an agony of grief, which sometimes reappears on the surface.'

At that instant the purveyor raised his eyes and rested them upon me; that glance made me quiver, so full was it of gloomy thought. But suddenly his face grew lively; he picked up the cut-glass stopper and put it, with a mechanical movement, into a decanter full of water that was near his plate, and then he turned to Monsieur Hermann and smiled. After all, that man, now beatified by gastronomical enjoyments, hadn't probably two ideas in his brain, and was thinking of nothing. Consequently I felt rather ashamed of wasting my powers of divination 'in anima vili'—of a doltish financier.

While I was thus making, at a dead loss, these phrenological observations, the worthy German had lined his nose with a good pinch of snuff and was now beginning his tale. It would be difficult to reproduce it in his own language, with his frequent interruptions and wordy digressions. Therefore, I now write it down in my own way; leaving out the faults of the Nuremburger, and taking only what his tale may have had of interest and poesy with the coolness of writers who forget to put on the title pages of their books: 'Translated from the German'.

THOUGHT AND ACT

Toward the end of Venemiaire, year VII, a republican period which in the present day corresponds to 20 October 1799, two young men, leaving Bonn in the early morning, had reached by nightfall the environs of Andernach, a small town standing on the left bank of the Rhine a few leagues from Coblentz. At that time the French army, commanded by Augereau, was manoeuvring before the Austrians, who then occupied the right bank of the river. The headquarters of the Republican division was at Coblentz, and one of the demi-brigades belonging to Augereau's corps was stationed at Andernach.

The two travellers were Frenchmen. At sight of their uniforms, blue mixed with white and faced with red velvet, their sabres, and above all their hats covered with a green varnished-cloth and adorned with a tricolour plume, even the German peasants had recognized army surgeons, a body of men of science and merit liked, for the most part, not only in our own army but also in the countries invaded by our troops. At this period many sons of good families taken from their medical studies by the recent conscription law due to General Jourdan, had naturally preferred to continue their studies on the battlefield rather than be restricted to mere military duty, little in keeping with their early education and their peaceful destinies. Men of science, pacific yet useful, these young men did actual good in the midst of so much misery, and formed a bond of sympathy with other men of science in the various countries through which the cruel civilization of the Republic passed.

The two young men were each provided with a pass and a commission as assistant-surgeon signed Coste and Bernadotte; and they were on their way to join the demi-brigade to which they were attached. Both belonged to moderately rich families in Beauvais, a town in which the gentle manners and loyalty of the provinces are transmitted as a species of birthright. Attracted to the theatre of war before the date at which they were required to begin their functions, they had travelled by diligence to Strasburg. Though maternal prudence had only allowed them a slender sum of money they thought themselves rich in possessing a few louis, an actual treasure in those days when assignats were reaching their lowest depreciation and gold was worth far more than silver. The two young surgeons, about twenty years of age at the most, yielded themselves up to the poesy of their situation with all the enthusiasm of youth. Between Strasburg and Bonn they had visited the Electorate and the banks of the Rhine as artists, philosophers, and observers. When a man's destiny is scientific he is, at their age, a being who is truly many-sided. Even in making love or in travelling, an assistant-surgeon should be gathering up the rudiments of his fortune or his coming fame.

The two young men had therefore given themselves wholly to that deep admiration which must affect all educated men on seeing the banks of the Rhine and the scenery of Suabia between Mayenne and Cologne, —a strong, rich, vigorously varied nature, filled with feudal memories, ever fresh and verdant, yet retaining at all points the imprints of fire and sword. Louis XIV and Turenne have cauterized that beautiful land. Here and there certain ruins bear witness to the pride or rather the foresight of the King of Versailles, who caused to be pulled down the ancient castles that once adorned this part of Germany. Looking at this marvellous country, covered with forests, where the picturesque charm of the middle ages abounds, though in ruins, we are able to conceive the German genius, its reverie, its mysticism.

The stay of the two friends at Bonn had the double purpose of science and pleasure. The grand hospital of the Gallo-Batavian army and of Augereau's division was established in the very palace of the Elector. These assistant-surgeons of recent date went there to see old comrades, to present their letters of recommendation to their medical chiefs, and to familiarize themselves with the first aspects of their profession. There, as elsewhere, they got rid of a few prejudices to which we cling so fondly in favour of the beauties of our native land. Surprised by the aspect of the columns of marble which adorn the Electoral Palace, they went about admiring the grandiose effects of German architecture, and finding everywhere new treasures both modern and antique.

From time to time the highways along which the two friends rode at leisure on their way to Andernach, led them over the crest of some granite hill that was higher than the rest. Thence, through a clearing of the forest or cleft in the rocky barrier, they caught sudden glimpses of the Rhine framed in stone or festooned with vigorous vegetation. The valleys, the forest paths, the trees exhaled that autumnal odour which induced to reverie; the wooded summits were beginning to gild and to take on the warm brown tones significant of age; the leaves were falling, but the skies were still azure and the dry roads lay like yellow lines along the landscape, just then illuminated by the oblique rays of the setting sun. At a mile and a half from Andernach the two friends walked their horses in silence, as if no war were devastating this beautiful land, while they followed a path made for the goats across the lofty walls of bluish granite between which foams the Rhine. Presently they descended by one of the declivities of the gorge, at the foot of which is placed the little town, seated coquettishly on the banks of the river and offering a convenient port to mariners.

'Germany is a beautiful country!' cried one of the two young men, who was named Prosper Magnan, at the moment when he caught sight of the painted houses of Andernach, pressed together like eggs in a basket, and separated only by trees, gardens, and flowers. Then he admired for a moment the pointed roofs with their projecting eaves, the wooden staircases, the galleries of a thousand peaceful dwellings, and the vessels swaying to the waves in the port.

[At the moment when Monsieur Hermann uttered the name of Prosper Magnan, my opposite neighbour seized the decanter, poured out a glass of water, and emptied it at a draught. This movement having attracted my attention, I thought I noticed a slight trembling of the hand and a moisture on the brow of the capitalist.

'What is that man's name?' I asked my neighbour.

'Taillefer,' she replied.

'Do you feel ill?' I said to him, observing that this strange personage was turning pale.

'Not at all,' he said with a polite gesture of thanks. 'I am listening,' he added, with a nod to the guests, who were all simultaneously looking at him.

'I have forgotten,' said Monsieur Hermann, 'the name of the other young man. But the confidences which Prosper Magnan subsequently made to me enabled me to know that his companion was dark, rather thin, and jovial. I will, if you please, call him Wilhelm, to give greater clearness to the tale I am about to tell you.'

The worthy German resumed his narrative after having, without the smallest regard for romanticism and local colour, baptized the young French surgeon with a Teutonic name.]

By the time the two young men reached Andernach the night was dark. Presuming that they would lose much time in looking for their chiefs and obtaining from them a military billet in a town already full of soldiers, they resolved to spend their last night of freedom at an inn standing some two or three hundred feet from Andernach, the rich colour of which, embellished by the fires of the setting sun, they had greatly admired from the summit of the hill above the town. Painted entirely red, this inn produced a most piquant effect in the landscape, whether by detaching itself from the general background of the town, or by contrasting its scarlet sides with the verdure of the surrounding foliage, and the gray-blue tints of the water. This house owed its name, the Red Inn, to this external decoration, imposed upon it, no doubt from time immemorial by the caprice of its founder. A mercantile superstition, natural enough to the different possessors of the building, far-famed among the sailors of the Rhine, had made them scrupulous to preserve the title.

Hearing the sound of horses' hoofs, the master of the Red Inn came out upon the threshold of his door.

'By heavens! Gentlemen,' he cried, 'a little later and you'd have had to sleep beneath the stars, like a good many more of your compatriots who are bivouacking on the other side of Andernach. Here every room is occupied. If you want to sleep in a good bed I have only my own room to offer you. As for your horses I can litter them down in a corner of the courtyard. The stable is full of people. Do these gentlemen come from France?' he added after a slight pause.

'From Bonn,' cried Prosper, 'and we have eaten nothing since morning.'

'Oh! As to provisions,' said the innkeeper, nodding his head, 'people come to the Red Inn for their wedding feast from thirty miles round. You shall have a princely meal, a Rhine fish! More, I need not say.'

After confiding their weary steeds to the care of the landlord, who vainly called to his hostler, the two young men entered the public room of the inn. Thick white clouds exhaled by a numerous company of smokers prevented them from at first recognizing the persons with whom they were thrown; but after sitting awhile near the table, with the patience practised by philosophical travellers who know the inutility of making a fuss, they distinguished through the vapours of tobacco the inevitable accessories of a German inn: the stove, the clock, the pots of beer, the long pipes, and here and there the eccentric physiognomies of Jews, or Germans, and the weather-beaten faces of mariners. The epaulets of several French officers were glittering through the mist, and the clank of spurs and sabres echoed incessantly from the brick floor. Some were playing cards, others argued, or held their tongues and ate, drank, or walked about. One stout little woman, wearing a black velvet cap, blue and silver stomacher, pincushion, bunch of keys, silver buckles, braided hair—all distinctive signs of the mistress of a German inn (a costume which has been so often depicted in coloured prints that it is too common to describe here),—well, this wife of the innkeeper kept the two friends alternately patient and impatient with remarkable ability.

Little by little the noise decreased, the various travellers retired to their rooms, the clouds of smoke dispersed. When places were set for the two young men, and the classic carp of the Rhine appeared upon the table, eleven o'clock was striking and the room was empty. The silence of night enabled the young surgeons to hear vaguely the noise their horses made in eating their provender, and the murmur of the waters of the Rhine, together with those indefinable sounds which always enliven an inn when filled with persons preparing to go to bed. Doors and windows are opened and shut, voices murmur vague words, and a few interpellations echo along the passages.

At this moment of silence and tumult the two Frenchmen and their landlord, who was boasting of Andernach, his inn, his cookery, the Rhine wines, the Republican army, and his wife, were all three listening with a sort of interest to the hoarse cries of sailors in a boat which appeared to be coming to the wharf.

The innkeeper, familiar no doubt with the guttural shouts of the boatmen, went out hastily, but presently returned conducting a short stout man, behind whom walked two sailors carrying a heavy valise and several packages. When these were deposited in the room, the short man took the valise and placed it beside him as he seated himself without ceremony at the same table as the surgeons.

'Go and sleep in your boat,' he said to the boatmen, 'as the inn is full. Considering all things, that is best.'

'Monsieur,' said the landlord to the new-comer, 'these are all the provisions I have left,' pointing to the supper served to the two Frenchmen. 'I haven't so much as another crust of bread nor a bone.'

'No sauer-kraut?'

'Not enough to put in my wife's thimble! As I had the honour to tell you just now, you can have no bed but the chair on which you are sitting, and no other chamber than this public room.'

At these words the little man cast upon the landlord, the room, and the two Frenchmen a look in which caution and alarm were equally expressed.

['Here,' said Monsieur Hermann, interrupting himself, 'I ought to tell you that we have never known the real name nor the history of this man; his papers showed that he came from Aix-la-Chapelle; he called himself Wahlenfer and said that he owned a rather extensive pin manufactory in the suburbs of Neuwied. Like all the manufacturers of that region, he wore a surtout coat of common cloth, waistcoat and breeches of dark green velveteen, stout boots, and a broad leather belt. His face was round, his manners frank and cordial; but during the evening he seemed unable to disguise altogether some secret apprehension or, possibly, some anxious care. The innkeeper's opinion has always been that this German merchant was fleeing his country. Later

I heard that his manufactory had been burned by one of those unfortunate chances so frequent in times of war. In spite of its anxious expression the man's face showed great kindliness. His features were handsome; and the whiteness of his stout throat was well set off by a black cravat, a fact which Wilhelm showed jestingly to Prosper.'

Here Monsieur Taillefer drank another glass of water.]

Prosper courteously proposed that the merchant should share their supper, and Wahlenfer accepted the offer without ceremony, like a man who feels himself able to return a civility. He placed his valise on the floor and put his feet on it, took off his hat and gloves and removed a pair of pistols from his belt; the landlord having by this time set a knife and fork for him, the three guests began to satisfy their appetites in silence. The atmosphere of this room was hot and the flies were so numerous that Prosper requested the landlord to open the window looking toward the outer gate, so as to change the air. This window was barricaded by an iron bar, the two ends of which were inserted into holes made in the window casings. For greater security, two bolts were screwed to each shutter. Prosper accidentally noticed the manner in which the landlord managed these obstacles and opened the window.

As I am now speaking of localities, this is the place to describe to you the interior arrangements of the inn; for, on an accurate knowledge of the premises depends an understanding of my tale. The public room in which the three persons I have named to you were sitting, had two outer doors. One opened on the main road to Andernach, which skirts the Rhine. In front of the inn was a little wharf, to which the boat hired by the merchant for his journey was moored. The other door opened upon the courtyard of the inn. This courtyard was surrounded by very high walls and was full, for the time being, of cattle and horses, the stables being occupied by human beings. The great gate leading into this courtyard had been so carefully barricaded that to save time the landlord had brought the merchant and sailors into the public room through the door opening on the roadway. After having opened the window, as requested by Prosper Magnan, he closed this door, slipped the iron bars into their places and ran the bolts. The landlord's room, where the two young surgeons were to sleep, adjoined the public room, and was separated by a somewhat thin partition from the kitchen, where the landlord and his wife intended, probably, to pass the night. The servant-woman had left the premises to find a lodging in some crib or hayloft. It is therefore easy to see that the kitchen, the landlord's chamber, and the public room were, to some extent, isolated from the rest of the house. In the courtyard were two large dogs, whose deep-toned barking showed vigilant and easily roused guardians.

'What silence! and what a beautiful night!' said Wilhelm, looking at the sky through the window, as the landlord was fastening the door.

The lapping of the river against the wharf was the only sound to be heard.

'Messieurs,' said the merchant, 'permit me to offer you a few bottles of wine to wash down the carp. We'll ease the fatigues of the day by drinking. From your manner and the state of your clothes, I judge that you have made, like me, a good bit of a journey to-day.'

The two friends accepted, and the landlord went out by a door through the kitchen to his cellar, situated, no doubt, under this portion of the building. When five venerable bottles which he presently brought back with him appeared on the table, the wife brought in the rest of the supper. She gave to the dishes and to the room generally the glance of a mistress, and then, sure of having attended to all the wants of the travellers, she returned to the kitchen.

The four men, for the landlord was invited to drink, did not hear her go to bed, but later, during the intervals of silence which came into their talk, certain strongly accentuated snores, made the more sonorous by the thin planks of the loft in which she had ensconced herself, made the guests laugh and also the husband. Towards midnight, when nothing remained on the table but biscuits, cheese, dried fruit, and good wine, the guests, chiefly the young Frenchmen, became communicative. The latter talked of their homes, their studies, and of the war. The conversation grew lively. Prosper Magnan brought a few tears to the merchant's eyes, when with the frankness and naivete of a good and tender nature, he talked of what his mother must be doing at that hour, while he was sitting drinking on the banks of the Rhine.

'I can see her,' he said, 'reading her prayers before she goes to bed. She won't forget me; she is certain to say to herself, "My poor Prosper; I wonder where he is now!" If she has won a few sous from her neighbours—your mother, perhaps,' he added, nudging Wilhelm's elbow—'she'll go and put them in the great red earthenware pot, where she is accumulating a sum sufficient to buy the thirty acres adjoining her little estate at Lescheville. Those thirty acres are worth at least sixty thousand francs. Such fine fields! Ah! if I had them I'd live all my days at Lescheville, without other ambition! How my father used to long for those thirty acres and the pretty brook which winds through the meadows! But he died without ever being able to buy them. Many's the time I've played there!'

'Monsieur Wahlenfer, haven't you also your "hoc erat in votis"?' asked Wilhelm.

'Yes, monsieur, but it came to pass, and now—'

The good man was silent, and did not finish his sentence.

'As for me,' said the landlord, whose face was rather flushed, 'I bought a field last spring, which I had been wanting for ten years.'

They talked thus like men whose tongues are loosened by wine, and they each took that friendly liking to the others of which we are never stingy on a journey; so that when the time came to separate for the night, Wilhelm offered his bed to the merchant.

'You can accept it without hesitation,' he said, 'for I can sleep with Prosper. It won't be the first, nor the last time either. You are our elder, and we ought to honour age!'

'Bah!' said the landlord, 'my wife's bed has several mattresses; take one off and put it on the floor.'

So saying, he went and shut the window, making all the noise that prudent operation demanded.

'I accept,' said the merchant; 'in fact I will admit,' he added, lowering his voice and looking at the two Frenchmen, 'that I desired it. My boatmen seem to me suspicious. I am not sorry to spend the night with two brave young men, two French soldiers, for, between ourselves, I have a hundred thousand francs in gold and diamonds in my valise.'

The friendly caution with which this imprudent confidence was received by the two young men seemed to reassure the German. The landlord assisted in taking off one of the mattresses, and when all was arranged for the best he bade them good-night and went off to bed.

The merchant and the surgeons laughed over the nature of their pillows. Prosper put his case of surgical instruments and that of Wilhelm under the end of his mattress to raise it and supply the place of a bolster, which was lacking. Wahlenfer, as a measure of precaution, put his valise under his pillow.

'We shall both sleep on our fortune,' said Prosper, 'you, on your gold; I, on my instruments. It remains to be seen whether my instruments will ever bring me the gold you have now acquired.'

'You may hope so,' said the merchant. 'Work and honesty can do everything; have patience, however.'

Wahlenfer and Wilhelm were soon asleep. Whether it was that his bed on the floor was hard, or that his great fatigue was a cause of sleeplessness, or that some fatal influence affected his soul, it is certain that Prosper Magnan continued awake. His thoughts unconsciously took an evil turn. His mind dwelt exclusively on the hundred thousand francs which lay beneath the merchant's pillow. To Prosper Magnan one hundred thousand francs was a vast and ready-made fortune. He began to employ it in a hundred different ways; he made castles in the air, such as we all make with eager delight during the moments preceding sleep, an hour when images rise in our minds confusedly, and often, in the silence of the night, thought acquires some magical power. He gratified his mother's wishes; he bought the thirty acres of meadow land; he married a young lady of Beauvais to whom his present want of fortune forbade him to aspire. With a hundred thousand francs he planned a lifetime of happiness; he saw himself prosperous, the father of a family, rich, respected in his province, and, possibly, mayor of Beauvais. His brain heated; he searched for means to turn his fictions to realities. He began with extraordinary ardour to plan a crime theoretically. While fancying the death of the merchant he saw distinctly the gold and the diamonds. His eyes were dazzled by them. His heart throbbed. Deliberation was, undoubtedly, already crime. Fascinated by that mass of gold he intoxicated himself morally by murderous arguments. He asked himself if that poor German had any need to live; he supposed the case of his never having existed. In short, he planned the crime in a manner to secure himself impunity. The other bank of the river was occupied by the Austrian army; below the windows lay a boat and boatman; he would cut the throat of that man, throw the body into the Rhine, and escape with the valise; gold would buy the boatman and he could reach the Austrians. He went so far as to calculate the professional ability he had reached in the use of instruments, so as to cut through his victim's throat without leaving him the chance for a single cry.

[Here Monsieur Taillefer wiped his forehead and drank a little water.]

Prosper rose slowly, making no noise. Certain of having waked no one, he dressed himself and went into the public room. There, with that fatal intelligence a man suddenly finds on some occasions within him, with that power of tact and will which is never lacking to prisoners or to criminals in whatever they undertake, he unscrewed the iron bars, slipped them from their places without the slightest noise, placed them against the wall, and opened the shutters, leaning heavily upon their hinges to keep them from creaking. The moon was shedding its pale pure light upon the scene, and he was thus enabled to faintly see into the room where Wilhelm and Wahlenfer were sleeping. There, he told me, he stood still for a moment. The throbbing of his heart was so strong, so deep, so sonorous, that he was terrified; he feared he could not act with coolness; his hands trembled; the soles of his feet seem planted on red-hot coal; but the execution of his plan was accompanied by such apparent good luck that he fancied he saw a species of predestination in this favour bestowed upon him by fate. He opened the window, returned to the bedroom, took his case of instruments, and selected the one most suitable to accomplish the crime.

'When I stood by the bed,' he said to me, 'I commended myself mechanically to God.'

At the moment when he raised his arm collecting all his strength, he heard a voice as it were within him; he thought he saw a light. He flung the instrument on his own bed and fled into the next room, and stood before the window. There, he conceived the utmost horror of himself. Feeling his virtue weak, fearing still to succumb to the spell that was upon him he sprang out upon the road and walked along the bank of the Rhine, pacing up and down like a sentinel before the inn. Sometimes he went as far as Andernach in his hurried tramp; often his feet led him up the slope he had descended on his way to the inn; and sometimes he lost sight of the inn and the window he had left open behind him. His object, he said, was to weary himself and so find sleep.

But, as he walked beneath the cloudless skies, beholding the stars, affected perhaps by the purer air of night and the melancholy lapping of the water, he fell into a reverie which brought him back by degrees to sane moral thoughts. Reason at last dispersed completely his momentary frenzy. The teachings of his education, its religious precepts, but above all, so he told me, the remembrance of his simple life beneath the parental roof drove out his wicked thoughts. When he returned to the inn after a long meditation to which he abandoned himself on the bank of the Rhine, resting his elbow on a rock, he could, he said to me, not have slept, but have watched untempted beside millions of gold. At the moment when his virtue rose proudly and vigorously from the struggle, he knelt down, with a feeling of ecstasy and happiness, and thanked God. He felt happy, light-hearted, content, as on the day of his first communion, when he thought himself worthy of the angels because he had passed one day without sinning in thought, or word, or deed.

He returned to the inn and closed the window without fearing to make a noise, and went to bed at once. His moral and physical lassitude was certain to bring him sleep. In a very short time after laying his head on his mattress, he fell into that first fantastic somnolence which precedes the deepest sleep. The senses then grew numb, and life is abolished by degrees; thoughts are incomplete, and the last quivering of our consciousness seems like a sort of reverie. 'How heavy the air is!' he thought; 'I seem to be breathing a moist vapour.' He explained this vaguely to himself by the difference which must exist between the atmosphere of the close room and the purer air by the river. But presently he heard a periodical noise, something like that made by drops of water falling from a robinet into a fountain. Obeying a feeling of panic terror he was about to rise and call the innkeeper and waken Wahlenfer and Wilhelm, but he suddenly remembered, alas! to his great misfortune, the tall wooden clock; he fancied the sound was that of the pendulum, and he fell asleep with that confused and indistinct perception.

['Do you want some water, Monsieur Taillefer?' said the master of the house, observing that the banker was mechanically pouring from an empty decanter.

Monsieur Hermann continued his narrative after the slight pause occasioned by this interruption.]

The next morning Prosper Magnan was awakened by a great noise. He seemed to hear piercing cries, and he felt that violent shuddering of the nerves which we suffer when on awaking we continue to feel a painful impression begun in sleep. A physiological fact then takes place within us, a start, to use the common expression, which has never been sufficiently observed, though it contains very curious phenomena for science. This terrible agony, produced, possibly, by the too sudden reunion of our two natures separated during sleep, is usually transient; but in the poor young surgeon's case it lasted, and even increased, causing him suddenly the most awful horror as he beheld a pool of blood between Wahlenfer's bed and his own mattress. The head of the unfortunate German lay on the ground; his body was still on the bed; all its blood had flowed out by the neck.

Seeing the eyes still open but fixed, seeing the blood which had stained his sheets and even his hands, recognizing his own surgical instrument beside him, Prosper Magnan fainted and fell into the pool of Wahlenfer's blood. 'It was,' he said to me, 'the punishment of my thoughts.' When he recovered consciousness he was in the public room, seated on a chair, surrounded by French soldiers, and in presence of a curious and observing crowd. He gazed stupidly at a Republican officer engaged in taking the testimony of several witnesses, and in writing down, no doubt, the 'proces-verbal'. He recognized the landlord, his wife, the two boatmen, and the servant of the Red Inn. The surgical instrument which the murderer had used—

[Here Monsieur Taillefer coughed, drew out his handkerchief to blow his nose, and wiped his forehead. These perfectly natural motions were noticed by me only; the other guests sat with their eyes fixed on Monsieur Hermann, to whom they were listening with a sort of avidity. The purveyor leaned his elbow on the table, put his head into his right hand and gazed fixedly at Hermann. From that moment he showed no other sign of emotion or interest, but his face remained passive and ghastly, as it was when I first saw him playing with the stopper of the decanter.]

The surgical instrument which the murderer had used was on the table with the case containing the rest of the instruments, together with Prosper's purse and papers. The gaze of the assembled crowd turned alternately from these convicting articles to the young man, who seemed to be dying and whose half-extinguished eyes apparently saw nothing. A confused murmur which was heard without proved the presence of a crowd, drawn to the neighbourhood of the inn by the news of the crime, and also perhaps by a desire to see the murderer. The step of the sentries placed beneath the windows of the public room and the rattle of their accoutrements could be heard above the talk of the populace; but the inn was closed and the courtyard was empty and silent.

Incapable of sustaining the glance of the officer who was gathering his testimony, Prosper Magnan suddenly felt his hand pressed by a man, and he raised his eyes to see who his protector could be in that crowd of enemies. He recognized by his uniform the surgeon-major of the demi-brigade then stationed at Andernach. The glance of that man was so piercing, so stern, that the poor young fellow shuddered, and suffered his head to fall on the back of his chair. A soldier put vinegar to his nostrils and he recovered consciousness. Nevertheless his haggard eyes were so devoid of life and intelligence that the surgeon said to the officer after feeling Prosper's pulse—

'Captain, it is impossible to question the man at this moment.'

'Very well! Take him away,' replied the captain, interrupting the surgeon, and addressing a corporal who stood behind the prisoner. 'You cursed coward!' he went on, speaking to Prosper in a low voice, 'try at least to walk firmly before these German curs, and save the honour of the Republic.'

This address seemed to wake up Prosper Magnan, who rose and made a few steps forward; but when the door was opened and he felt the fresh air and saw the crowd before him, he staggered and his knees gave way under him.

'This coward of a sawbones deserves a dozen deaths! Get on!' cried the two soldiers who had him in charge, lending him their arms to support him.

'There he is! —Oh, the villain! the coward! Here he is! There he is!'

These cries seemed to be uttered by a single voice, the tumultuous voice of the crowd which followed him with insults and swelled at every step. During the passage from the inn to the prison, the noise made by the tramping of the crowd and the soldiers, the murmur of the various colloquies, the sight of the sky, the coolness of the air, the aspect of Andernach and the shimmering of the waters of the Rhine—these impressions came to the soul of the young man vaguely, confusedly, torpidly, like all the sensations he had felt since his waking. There were moments, he said, when he thought he was no longer living.

I was then in prison. Enthusiastic, as we all are at twenty years of age, I wished to defend my country, and I commanded a company of free lances, which I had organized in the vicinity of Andernach. A few days before these events I had fallen plump, during the night, into a French detachment of eight hundred men. We were two hundred at the most. My scouts had sold me. I was thrown into the prison of Andernach, and they talked of shooting me, as a warning to intimidate others. The French talked also of reprisals. My father, however, obtained a reprieve for three days to give him time to see General Augereau, whom he knew, and ask for my pardon, which was granted. Thus it happened that I saw Prosper Magnan when he was brought to the prison. He inspired me with the profoundest pity. Though pale, distracted, and covered with blood, his whole countenance had a character of truth and innocence which struck me forcibly. To me his long fair hair and clear blue eyes seemed German. A true image of my hapless country. I felt he was a victim and not a murderer. At the moment when he passed beneath my window he chanced to cast about him the painful, melancholy smile of an insane man who suddenly recovers for a time a fleeting gleam of reason. That smile was assuredly not the smile of a murderer. When I saw the jailer I questioned him about his new prisoner.

'He has not spoken since I put him in his cell,' answered the man. 'He is sitting down with his head in his hands and is either sleeping or reflecting about his crime. The French say he'll get his reckoning tomorrow morning and be shot in twenty-four hours.'

That evening I stopped short under the window of the prison during the short time I was allowed to take exercise in the prison yard. We talked together, and he frankly related to me his strange affair, replying with evident truthfulness to my various questions.

After that first conversation I no longer doubted his innocence; I asked, and obtained the favour of staying several hours with him. I saw him again at intervals, and the poor lad let me in without concealment to all his thoughts. He believed himself both innocent and guilty. Remembering the horrible temptation which he had had the strength to resist, he feared he might have done in sleep, in a fit of somnambulism, the crime he had dreamed of awake.

'But your companion?' I said to him.

'Oh!' he cried eagerly. 'Wilhelm is incapable of—'

He did not even finish his sentence. At that warm defence, so full of youth and manly virtue, I pressed his hand.

'When he woke,' continued Prosper, 'he must have been terrified and lost his head; no doubt he fled.'

'Without awaking you?' I said. 'Then surely your defence is easy; Wahlenfer's valise cannot have been stolen.'

Suddenly he burst into tears.

'Oh, yes!' he cried, 'I am innocent! I have not killed a man! I remember my dreams. I was playing at base with my schoolmates. I couldn't have cut off the head of a man while I dreamed I was running.'

Then, in spite of these gleams of hope, which gave him at times some calmness, he felt a remorse which crushed him. He had, beyond all question, raised his arm to kill that man. He judged himself; and he felt that his heart was not innocent after committing that crime in his mind.

'And yet, I am good!' he cried. 'Oh, my poor mother! Perhaps at this moment she is cheerfully playing boston with the neighbours in her little tapestry salon. If she knew that I had raised my hand to murder a man—oh! she would die of it! And I am in prison, accused of committing that crime! If I have not killed a man, I have certainly killed my mother!'

Saying these words he wept no longer; he was seized by that

short and rapid madness known to the men of Picardy; he sprang to the wall, and if I had not caught him, he would have dashed out his brains against it.

'Wait for your trial,' I said. 'You are innocent, you will certainly be acquitted; think of your mother.'

'My mother!' he cried frantically, 'she will hear of the accusation before she hears anything else,—it is always so in little towns; and the shock will kill her. Besides, I am not innocent. Must I tell you the whole truth? I feel that I have lost the virginity of my conscience.'

After that terrible avowal he sat down, crossed his arms on his breast, bowed his head upon it, gazing gloomily on the ground. At this instant the turnkey came to ask me to return to my room. Grieved to leave my companion at a moment when his discouragement was so deep, I pressed him in my arms with friendship, saying—

Have patience; all may yet go well. If the voice of an honest man can still your doubts, believe that I esteem you and trust you. Accept my friendship, and rest upon my heart, if you cannot find peace in your own.'

The next morning a corporal's guard came to fetch the young surgeon at nine o'clock. Hearing the noise made by the soldiers, I stationed myself at my window. As the prisoner crossed the courtyard, he cast his eyes up to me. Never shall I forget that look, full of thoughts, presentiments, resignation, and I know not what sad, melancholy grace. It was, as it were, a silent but intelligible last will by which a man bequeathed his lost existence to his only friend. The night must have been very hard, very solitary for him; and yet, perhaps, the pallor of his face expressed a stoicism gathered from some new sense of self-respect. Perhaps he felt that his remorse had purified him, and believed that he had blotted out his fault by his anguish and his shame. He now walked with a firm step, and since the previous evening he had washed away the blood with which he was, involuntarily, stained.

'My hands must have dabbled in it while I slept, for I am always a restless sleeper,' he had said to me in tones of horrible despair.

I learned that he was on his way to appear before the council of war. The division was to march on the following morning, and the commanding officer did not wish to leave Andernach without inquiry into the crime on the spot where it had been committed. I remained in the utmost anxiety during the time the council lasted. At last, about midday, Prosper Magnan was brought back. I was then taking my usual walk; he saw me, and came and threw himself into my arms.

'Lost!' he said, 'lost, without hope! Here, to all the world, I am a murderer.' He raised his head proudly. 'This injustice restores to me my innocence. My life would always have been wretched; my death leaves me without reproach. But is there a future?'

The whole eighteenth century was in that sudden question. He remained thoughtful.

'Tell me,' I said to him, 'how you answered. What did they ask you? Did you not relate the simple facts as you told them to me?'

He looked at me fixedly for a moment; then, after that awful pause, he answered with feverish excitement—

'First they asked me, "Did you leave the inn during the night?" I said, "Yes." "How?" I answered, "By the window." "Then you must have taken great precautions; the innkeeper heard no noise.:" I was stupefied. The sailors said they saw me walking, first to Andernach, then to the forest. I made many trips, they said, no doubt to bury the gold and diamonds. The valise had not been found. My remorse still held me dumb. When I wanted to speak, a pitiless voice cried out to me, "You meant to commit that crime!" All was against me, even myself. They asked me about my comrade, and I completely exonerated him. Then they said to me: "The crime must lie between you, your comrade, the innkeeper, and his wife. This morning all the windows and doors were found securely fastened." "At those words," continued the poor fellow, "I had neither voice, nor strength, nor soul to answer. More sure of my comrade than I could be of myself, I could not accuse him. I saw that we were both thought equally guilty of the murder, and that I was considered the most clumsy. I tried to explain the crime by somnambulism, and so protect my friend; but there I rambled and contradicted myself. No, I am lost. I read my condemnation in the eyes of my judges. They smiled incredulously. All is over. No more uncertainty. Tomorrow I shall be shot. I am not thinking of myself," he went on after a pause, "but of my poor mother." Then he stopped, looked up to heaven, and shed no tears; his eyes were dry and strongly convulsed. "Frederic—"'

['Ah! true,' cried Monsieur Hermann, with an air of triumph. 'Yes, the other's name was Frederic, Frederic! I remember now!'

My neighbour touched my foot, and made me a sign to look at Monsieur Taillefer. The former purveyor had negligently dropped his hand over his eyes, but between the interstices of his fingers we thought we caught a darkling flame proceeding from them.

'Hein?' she said in my ear, 'what if his name were Frederic?'

I answered with a glance, which said to her: 'Silence!'

Hermann continued:]

'Frederic!' cried the young surgeon, 'Frederic basely deserted me. He must have been afraid. Perhaps he is still hidden in the inn, for our horses were both in the courtyard this morning. What an incomprehensible mystery!' he went on, after a moment's silence. 'Somnambulism! somnambulism? I never had but one attack in my life, and that was when I was six years old. Must I go from this earth,' he cried, striking the ground with his foot, 'carrying with me all there is of friendship in the world? Shall I die a double death, doubting a fraternal love begun when we were only five years old, and continued through school and college? Where is Frederic?'

He wept. Can it be that we cling more to a sentiment than to life?

'Let us go in,' he said. 'I prefer to be in my cell. I do not wish to be seen weeping. I shall go courageously to death, but I cannot play the heroic at all moments; I own I regret my beautiful young life. All last night I could not sleep; I remembered the scenes of my childhood; I fancied I was running in the fields. Ah! I had a future,' he said, suddenly interrupting himself, 'and now, twelve men, a sub-lieutenant shouting "Carry-arms, aim, fire!" a roll of drums, and infamy! That's my future now. Oh! there must be a God, or it would all be too senseless.'

Then he took me in his arms and pressed me to him with all his strength.

'You are the last man, the last friend to whom I can show my soul. You will be set at liberty, you will see your mother! I don't know whether you are rich or poor, but no matter! you are all the world to me. They won't fight always, "ceux-ci". Well, when there's peace, will you go to Beauvais? If my mother has survived the fatal news of my death, you will find her there. Say to her the comforting words, "He was innocent!" She will believe you. I am going to write to her; but you must take her my last look; you must tell her that you were the last man whose hand I pressed. Oh, she'll love you, the poor woman! you, my last friend. Here,' he said, after a moment's silence, during which he was overcome by the weight of his recollections, 'all, officers and soldiers, are unknown to me; I am an object of horror to them. If it were not for you my innocence would be a secret between God and myself.'

I swore to sacredly fulfil his last wishes. My words, the emotion I showed touched him. Soon after that the soldiers came to take him again before the council of war. He was condemned to death. I am ignorant of the formalities that followed or accompanied this judgment, nor do I know whether the young surgeon defended his life or not; but he expected to be executed on the following day, and he spent the night in writing to his mother.

'We shall both be free to-day,' he said, smiling, when I went to see him the next morning. 'I am told that the general has signed your pardon.'

I was silent, and looked at him closely so as to carve his features, as it were, on my memory. Presently an expression of disgust crossed his face.

'I have been very cowardly,' he said. 'During all last night I begged for mercy of these walls,' and he pointed to the sides of his dungeon. 'Yes, yes, I howled with despair, I rebelled, I suffered the most awful moral agony—I was alone! Now I think of what others will say of me. Courage is a garment to put on. I desire to go decently to death, therefore—'

A DOUBLE RETRIBUTION

'Oh, stop! stop!' cried the young lady who had asked for this history, interrupting the narrator suddenly. 'Say no more; let me remain in uncertainty and believe that he was saved. If I hear now that he was shot I shall not sleep all night. Tomorrow you shall tell me the rest.'

We rose from the table. My neighbour in accepting Monsieur Hermann's arm, said to him—

'I suppose he was shot, was he not?'

'Yes. I was present at the execution.'

'Oh! monsieur,' she said, 'how could you—'

'He desired it, madame. There was something really dreadful in following the funeral of a living man, a man my heart cared for, an innocent man! The poor young fellow never ceased to look at me. He seemed to live only in me. He wanted, he said, that I should carry to his mother his last sigh.'

'And did you?'

'At the peace of Amiens I went to France, for the purpose of taking to the mother those blessed words, "He was innocent." I religiously undertook that pilgrimage. But Madame Magnan had died of consumption. It was not without deep emotion that I burned the letter of which I was the bearer. You will perhaps smile at my German imagination, but I see a drama of sad sublimity in the eternal secrecy which engulfed those parting words cast between two graves, unknown to all creation, like the cry uttered in a desert by some lonely traveller whom a lion seizes.'

'And if,' I said, interrupting him, 'you were brought face to face with a man now in this room, and were told, "This is the murderer!" would not that be another drama? And what would you do?'

Monsieur Hermann looked for his hat and went away.

'You are behaving like a young man, and very heedlessly,' said my neighbour. 'Look at Taillefer!—there, seated on that sofa at the corner of the fireplace. Mademoiselle Fanny is offering him a cup of coffee. He smiles. Would a murderer to whom that tale must have been torture, present so calm a face? Isn't his whole air patriarchal?'

'Yes; but go and ask him if he went to the war in Germany,' I said.

'Why not?'

And with that audacity which is seldom lacking to women when some action attracts them, or their minds are impelled by curiosity, my neighbour went up to the purveyor.

'Were you ever in Germany?' she asked.

Taillefer came near dropping his cup and saucer.

'I, madame? No, never.'

'What are you talking about, Taillefer?' said our host,

interrupting him. 'Were you not in the commissariat during the campaign of Wagram?'

'Ah, true!' replied Taillefer, 'I was there at that time.'

'You are mistaken,' said my neighbour, returning to my side, 'that's a good man.'

'Well,' I cried, 'before the end of this evening, I will hunt that murderer out of the slough in which he is hiding.'

Every day, before our eyes, a moral phenomenon of amazing profundity takes place which is, nevertheless, so simple as never to be noticed. If two men meet in a salon, one of whom has the right to hate or despise the other, whether from a knowledge of some private and latent fact which degrades him, or of a secret condition, or even of a coming revenge, those two men divine each other's souls, and are able to measure the gulf which separates or ought to separate them. They observe each other unconsciously; their minds are preoccupied by themselves; through their looks, their gestures, an indefinable emanation of their thought transpires; there's a magnet between them. I don't know which has the strongest power of attraction, vengeance or crime, hatred or insult. Like a priest who cannot consecrate the host in presence of an evil spirit, each is ill at ease and distrustful; one is polite, the other surly, but I know not which; one colours or turns pale, the other trembles. Often the avenger is as cowardly as the victim. Few men have the courage to invoke an evil, even when just or necessary, and men are silent or forgive a wrong from hatred of uproar or fear of some tragic ending.

This introsusception of our souls and our sentiments created a mysterious struggle between Taillefer and myself. Since the first inquiry I had put to him during Monsieur Hermann's narrative, he had steadily avoided my eye. Possibly he avoided those of all the other guests. He talked with the youthful, inexperienced daughter of the banker, feeling, no doubt, like many other criminals, a need of drawing near to innocence, hoping to find rest there. But, though I was a long distance from him, I heard him, and my piercing eye fascinated his. When he thought he could watch me unobserved our eyes met, and his eyelids dropped immediately.

Weary of this torture, Taillefer seemed determined to put an end to it by sitting down at a card-table. I at once went to bet on his adversary; hoping to lose my money. The wish was granted; the player left the table and I took his place, face to face with the murderer.

'Monsieur,' I said, while he dealt the cards, 'may I ask if you are Monsieur Frederic Taillefer, whose family I know very well at Beauvais?'

'Yes, monsieur,' he answered.

He dropped the cards, turned pale, put his hands to his head and rose, asking one of the bettors to take his hand.

'It is too hot here,' he cried, 'I fear—'

He did not end the sentence. His face expressed intolerable suffering, and he went out hastily. The master of the house followed him and seemed to take an anxious interest in his condition. My neighbour and I looked at each other, but I saw a tinge of bitter sadness or reproach upon her countenance.

'Do you think your conduct is merciful?' she asked, drawing me to the embrasure of a window just as I was leaving the card-table, having lost all my money. 'Would you accept the power of reading hearts? Why not leave things to human justice or divine justice? We may escape one but we cannot escape the other. Do you think the privilege of a judge of the Court of Assizes so much to be envied? You have almost done the work of an executioner.'

'After sharing and stimulating my curiosity, why are you now lecturing me on morality?'

'You have made me reflect,' she answered.

'So, then, peace to villains, war to the sorrowful, and let's deify gold! However, we will drop the subject,' I added, laughing. 'Do you see that young girl who is just entering the salon?'

'Yes, what of her?'

'I met her, three days ago, at the ball of the Neapolitan ambassador, and I am passionately in love with her. For pity's sake tell me her name. No one was able—'

'That is Mademoiselle Victorine Taillefer.'

I grew dizzy.

'Her step-mother,' continued my neighbour, 'has lately taken her from a convent, where she was finishing, rather late in the day, her education. For a long time her father refused to recognize her. She comes here for the first time. She is very beautiful and very rich.'

These words were accompanied by a sardonic smile.

At this moment we heard violent, but smothered outcries; they seemed to come from a neighbouring apartment and to be echoed faintly back through the garden.

'Isn't that the voice of Monsieur Taillefer?' I said.

We gave our full attention to the noise; a frightful moaning reached our ears. The wife of the banker came hurriedly towards us and closed the window.

'Let us avoid a scene,' she said. 'If Mademoiselle Taillefer hears her father, she might be thrown into hysterics.'

The banker now re-entered the salon, looked round for Victorine, and said a few words in her ear. Instantly the young girl uttered a cry, ran to the door, and disappeared. This event produced a great sensation. The card-players paused. Every one questioned his neighbour. The murmur of voices swelled, and groups gathered.

'Can Monsieur Taillefer be—' I began.

'—dead?' said my sarcastic neighbour. 'You would wear the gayest mourning, I fancy!'

'But what has happened to him?'

'The poor dear man,' said the mistress of the house, 'is subject to attacks of a disease the name of which I never can remember, though Monsieur Brousson has often told it to me; and he has just been seized with one.'

'What is the nature of the disease?' asked an examining judge.

'Oh, it is something terrible, monsieur,' she replied. 'The doctors know no remedy. It causes the most dreadful suffering. One day, while the unfortunate man was staying at my country-house, he had an attack, and I was obliged to go away and stay with a neighbour to avoid hearing him; his cries were terrible; he tried to kill himself; his daughter was obliged to have him put into a strait-jacket and fastened to his bed. The poor man declares there are live animals in his head gnawing his brain; every nerve quivers with horrible shooting pains, and he writhes in torture. He suffers so much in his head that he did not even feel the moxas they used formerly to apply to relieve it; but Monsieur Brousson, who is now his physician, has forbidden that remedy, declaring that the trouble is a nervous affection, an inflammation of the nerves, for which leeches should be applied to the neck, and opium to the head. As a result, the attacks are not so frequent; they appear now only about once a year, and always late in the autumn. When he recovers, Taillefer says repeatedly that he would far rather die than endure such torture.'

'Then he must suffer terribly!' said a broker, considered a wit, who was present.

'Oh,' continued the mistress of the house, 'last year he nearly died in one of these attacks. He had gone alone to his country-house on pressing business. For want, perhaps, of immediate help, he lay twenty-two hours stiff and stark as though he were dead. A very hot bath was all that saved him.'

'It must be a species of lockjaw,' said one of the guests.

'I don't know,' she answered. 'He got the disease in the army nearly thirty years ago. He says it was caused by a splinter of wood entering his head from a shot on board a boat. Brousson hopes to cure him. They say the English have discovered a mode of treating the disease with prussic acid—'

At that instant a still more piercing cry echoed through the house, and froze us with horror.

'There! that is what I listened to all day long last year,' said the banker's wife. 'It made me jump in my chair and rasped my nerves dreadfully. But, strange to say, poor Taillefer, though he suffers untold agony, is in no danger of dying. He eats and drinks as well as ever during even short cessations of the pain—nature is so queer! A German doctor told him it was a form of gout in the head, and that agrees with Brousson's opinion.'

I left the group around the mistress of the house and went away. On the staircase I met Mademoiselle Taillefer, whom a footman had come to fetch.

'Oh!' she said to me, weeping, 'what has my poor father ever done to deserve such suffering? —so kind as he is!'

I accompanied her downstairs and assisted her in getting into the carriage, and there I saw her father bent almost double.

Mademoiselle Taillefer tried to stifle his moans by putting her handkerchief to his mouth; unhappily he saw me; his face became even more distorted, a convulsive cry rent the air, and he gave me a dreadful look as the carriage rolled away.

That dinner, that evening exercised a cruel influence on my life and on my feelings. I loved Mademoiselle Taillefer, precisely, perhaps, because honour and decency forbade me to marry the daughter of a murderer, however good a husband and father he might be. A curious fatality impelled me to visit those houses where I knew I could meet Victorine; often, after giving myself my word of honour to renounce the happiness of seeing her, I found myself that same evening beside her. My struggles were great. Legitimate love, full of chimerical remorse, assumed the colour of a criminal passion. I despised myself for bowing to Taillefer when, by chance, he accompanied his daughter, but I bowed to him all the same.

Alas! for my misfortune Victorine is not only a pretty girl, she is also educated, intelligent, full of talent and of charm, without the slightest pedantry or the faintest tinge of assumption. She converses with reserve, and her nature has a melancholy grace which no one can resist. She loves me, or at least she lets me think so; she has a certain smile which she keeps for me alone; for me, her voice grows softer still. Oh, yes! she loves me! But she adores her father; she tells me of his kindness, his gentleness, his excellent qualities. Those praises are so many dagger-thrusts with which she stabs me to the heart.

One day I came near to making myself the accomplice, as it were, of the crime which led to the opulence of the Taillefer family. I was on the point of asking the father for Victorine's hand. But I fled; I travelled; I went to Germany, to Andernach; and then—I returned! I found Victorine pale, and thinner; if I had seen her well in health and gay, I should certainly have been saved. Instead of which my love burst out again with untold violence. Fearing that my scruples might degenerate into monomania, I resolved to convoke a sanhedrin of sound consciences, and obtain from them some light on this problem of high morality and philosophy,—a problem which had been, as we shall see, still further complicated since my return.

Two days ago, therefore, I collected those of my friends to whom I attribute most delicacy, probity, and honour. I invited two Englishmen, the secretary of an embassy, and a puritan; a former minister, now a mature statesman; a priest, an old man; also my former guardian, a simple-hearted being who rendered so loyal a guardianship account that the memory of it is still green at the Palais; besides these, there were present a judge, a lawyer, and a notary, in short, all social opinions, and all practical virtues.

We began by dining well, talking well, and making some noise; then, at dessert, I related my history candidly, and asked for advice, concealing, of course, the Taillefer name.

A profound silence suddenly fell upon the company. Then the notary took leave. He had, he said, a deed to draw.

The wine and the good dinner had reduced my former guardian to silence; in fact I was obliged later in the evening to put him under guardianship, to make sure of no mishap to him on his way home.

'I understand!' I cried. 'By not giving an opinion you tell me energetically enough what I ought to do.'

On this there came a stir throughout the assembly.

A capitalist who had subscribed for the children and tomb of General Foy exclaimed—

'Like Virtue's self, a crime has its degrees.'

'Rash tongue!' said the former minister, in a low voice, nudging me with his elbow.

'Where's your difficulty?' asked a duke whose fortune is derived from the estates of stubborn Protestants, confiscated on the revocation of the Edict of Nantes.

The lawyer rose, and said—

'In law, the case submitted to us presents no difficulty. Monsieur le duc is right!' cried the legal organ. 'There are time limitations. Where should we all be if we had to search into the origin of fortunes? This is simply an affair of conscience. If you must absolutely carry the case before some tribunal, go to that of the confessional.'

The Code incarnate ceased speaking, sat down, and drank a glass of champagne. The man charged with the duty of explaining the gospel, the good priest, rose.

'God has made us all frail beings,' he said firmly. 'If you love the heiress of that crime, marry her; but content yourself with the property she derives from her mother; give that of the father to the poor.'

'But,' cried one of those pitiless hair-splitters who are often to be met with in the world, 'perhaps the father could make a rich marriage only because he was rich himself; consequently, the marriage was the fruit of the crime.'

'This discussion is, in itself, a verdict. There are some things on which a man does not deliberate,' said my former guardian, who thought to enlighten the assembly with a flash of inebriety.

'Yes!' said the secretary of an embassy.

'Yes!' said the priest.

But the two men did not mean the same thing.

A 'doctrinaire', who had missed his election to the Chamber by one hundred and fifty votes out of one hundred and fifty-five, here rose.

'Messieurs,' he said, 'this phenomenal incident of intellectual nature is one of those which stand out vividly from the normal condition to which sobriety is subjected. Consequently the decision to be made ought to be the spontaneous act of our consciences, a sudden conception, a prompt inward verdict, a fugitive shadow of our mental apprehension, much like the flashes of sentiment which constitute taste. Let us vote.'

'Let us vote!' cried all my guests.

I have each two balls, one white, one red. The white, symbol of virginity, was to forbid the marriage; the red ball sanctioned it. I myself abstained from voting, out of delicacy.

My friends were seventeen in number; nine was therefore the majority. Each man put his ball into the wicker basket with a narrow throat, used to hold the numbered balls when card-players draw for their places at pool. We were all roused to a more or less keen curiosity; for this balloting to clarify morality was certainly original. Inspection of the ballot-box showed the presence of nine white balls! The result did not surprise me; but it came into my heard to count the young men of my own age whom I had brought to sit in judgment. These casuists were precisely nine in number; they all had the same thought.

'Oh, oh!' I said to myself, 'here is secret unanimity to forbid the marriage, and secret unanimity to sanction it! How shall I solve that problem?'

'Where does the father-in-law live?' asked one my school-friends, heedlessly, being less sophisticated than the others.

'There's no longer a father-in-law,' I replied. 'Hitherto, my conscience has spoken plainly enough to make your verdict superfluous. If today its voice is weakened, here is the cause of my cowardice. I received, about two months ago, this all-seducing letter.'

And I showed them the following invitation, which I took from my pocket-book—

'You are invited to be present at the funeral procession, burial services, and interment of Monsieur Jean-Frederic Taillefer, of the house of Taillefer and Company, formerly Purveyor of Commissary-meats, in his lifetime chevalier of the Legion of Honour, and of the Golden Spur, captain of the first company of the Grenadiers of the National Guard of Paris, deceased, May 1st, at his residence, rue Joubert; which will take place at, etc., etc.

'On the part of, etc.'

'Now, what am I do to?' I continued; 'I will put the question before you in a broad way. There is undoubtedly a sea of blood in Mademoiselle Taillefer's estates; her inheritance from her father is a vast Aceldama. I know that. But Prosper Magnan left no heirs; but, again, I have been unable to discover the family of the merchant who was murdered at Andernach. To whom therefore can I restore that fortune? And ought it to be wholly restored? Have I the right to betray a secret surprised by me,—to add a murdered head to the dowry of an innocent girl, to give her for the rest of her life bad dreams, to deprive her of all her illusions, and say, "Your gold is stained with blood"? I have borrowed the "Dictionary of Cases of Conscience" from an old ecclesiastic, but I can find nothing there to solve my doubts. Shall I found pious masses for the repose of the souls of Prosper Magnan, Wahlenfer, and Taillefer? Here we are in the middle of the nineteenth century! Shall I build a hospital, or institute a prize for virtue? A prize for virtue would be given to scoundrels; and as for hospitals, they seem to me to have become in these days the protectors of vice. Besides, such charitable actions, more or less profitable to vanity, do they constitute reparation?— and to whom do I owe reparation? But I love; I love passionately. My love is my life. If I, without apparent motive, suggest to a young girl accustomed to luxury, to elegance, to a life fruitful of all enjoyments of art, a young girl who loves to idly listen at the opera to Rossini's music,—if to her I should propose that she deprive herself of fifteen hundred thousand francs in favour of broken-down old men, or scrofulous paupers, she would turn her back on me and laugh, or her confidential friend would tell her that I'm a crazy jester. If in an ecstasy of love, I should paint to her the charms of a modest life, and a little home on the banks of the Loire; if I were to ask her to sacrifice her Parisian life on the altar of our love, it would be, in the first place, a virtuous lie; in the next, I might only be opening the way to some painful experience; I might lose the heart of a girl who loves society, and balls, and personal adornment, and me for the time being. Some slim and jaunty officer, with a well-frizzed moustache, who can play the piano, quote Lord Byron, and ride a horse elegantly, may get her away from me. What shall I do? For Heaven's sake, give me some advice!'

The honest man, that species of puritan not unlike the father of Jeannie Deans, of whom I have already told you, and who, up to the present moment hadn't uttered a word, shrugged his shoulders, as he looked at me and said—

'Idiot! Why did you ask him if he came from Beauvais?''

7

THE PURSE

To Sofka

'Have you observed, mademoiselle, that the painters and sculptors of the Middle Ages, when they placed two figures in adoration, one on each side of a fair Saint, never failed to give them a family likeness? When you here see your name among those that are dear to me, and under whose auspices I place my works, remember that touching harmony, and you will see in this not so much an act of homage as an expression of the brotherly affection of your devoted servant,'

—'DE BALZAC.'

For souls to whom effusiveness is easy there is a delicious hour that falls when it is not yet night, but is no longer day; the twilight gleam throws softened lights or tricksy reflections on every object, and favours a dreamy mood which vaguely weds itself to the play of light and shade. The silence which generally prevails at that time makes it particularly dear to artists, who grow contemplative, stand a few paces back from the pictures on which they can no longer work, and pass judgement on them, rapt by the subject whose most recondite meaning then flashes on the inner eye of genius. He who has never stood pensive by a friend's side in such an hour of poetic dreaming can hardly understand its inexpressible soothingness. Favoured by the clear-obscure, the material skill employed by art to produce illusion entirely disappears. If the work is a picture, the figures represented seem to speak and walk; the shade is shadow, the light is day; the flesh lives, eyes move, blood flows in their veins, and stuffs have a changing sheen. Imagination helps the realism of every detail, and only sees the beauties of the work. At that hour illusion reigns despotically; perhaps it wakes at nightfall! Is not illusion a sort of night to the mind, which we people with dreams? Illusion then unfolds its wings, it bears the soul aloft to the world of fancies, a world full of voluptuous imaginings, where the artist forgets the real world, yesterday and the morrow, the future—everything down to its miseries, the good and the evil alike.

At this magic hour a young painter, a man of talent, who saw in art nothing but Art itself, was perched on a step-ladder which helped him to work at a large high painting, now nearly finished. Criticizing himself, honestly admiring himself, floating on the current of his thoughts, he then lost himself in one of those meditative moods which ravish and elevate the soul, soothe it, and comfort it. His reverie had no doubt lasted a long time. Night fell. Whether he meant to come down from his perch, or whether he made some ill-judged movement, believing himself to be on the floor—the event did not allow of his remembering exactly the cause of his accident—he fell, his head struck a footstool, he lost consciousness and lay motionless during a space of time of which he knew not the length.

A sweet voice roused him from the stunned condition into which he had sunk. When he opened his eyes the flash of a bright light made him close them again immediately; but through the mist that veiled his senses he heard the whispering of two women, and felt two young, two timid hands on which his head was resting. He soon recovered consciousness, and by the light of an old-fashioned

Argand lamp he could make out the most charming girl's face he had ever seen, one of those heads which are often supposed to be a freak of the brush, but which to him suddenly realized the theories of the ideal beauty which every artist creates for himself and whence his art proceeds. The features of the unknown belonged, so to say, to the refined and delicate type of Prudhon's school, but had also the poetic sentiment which Girodet gave to the inventions of his phantasy. The freshness of the temples, the regular arch of the eyebrows, the purity of outline, the virginal innocence so plainly stamped on every feature of her countenance, made the girl a perfect creature. Her figure was slight and graceful, and frail in form. Her dress, though simple and neat, revealed neither wealth nor penury.

As he recovered his senses, the painter gave expression to his admiration by a look of surprise, and stammered some confused thanks. He found a handkerchief pressed to his forehead, and above the smell peculiar to a studio, he recognized the strong odour of ether, applied no doubt to revive him from his fainting fit. Finally he saw an old woman, looking like a marquise of the old school, who held the lamp and was advising the young girl.

'Monsieur,' said the younger woman in reply to one of the questions put by the painter during the few minutes when he was still under the influence of the vagueness that the shock had produced in his ideas, 'my mother and I heard the noise of your fall on the floor, and we fancied we heard a groan. The silence following on the crash alarmed us, and we hurried up. Finding the key in the latch, we happily took the liberty of entering, and we found you lying motionless on the ground. My mother went to fetch what was needed to bathe your head and revive you. You have cut your forehead—there. Do you feel it?'

'Yes, I do now,' he replied.

'Oh, it will be nothing,' said the old mother. 'Happily your head rested against this lay-figure.'

'I feel infinitely better,' replied the painter. 'I need nothing further but a hackney cab to take me home. The porter's wife will go for one.'

He tried to repeat his thanks to the two strangers; but at each sentence the elder lady interrupted him, saying, 'Tomorrow, monsieur, pray be careful to put on leeches, or to be bled, and drink a few cups of something healing. A fall may be dangerous.'

The young girl stole a look at the painter and at the pictures in the studio. Her expression and her glances revealed perfect propriety; her curiosity seemed rather absence of mind, and her eyes seemed to speak the interest which women feel, with the most engaging spontaneity, in everything which causes us suffering. The two strangers seemed to forget the painter's works in the painter's mishap. When he had reassured them as to his condition they left, looking at him with an anxiety that was equally free from insistence and from familiarity, without asking any indiscreet questions, or trying to incite him to any wish to visit them. Their proceedings all bore the hall-mark of natural refinement and good taste. Their noble and simple manners at first made no great impression on the painter, but subsequently, as he recalled all the details of the incident, he was greatly struck by them.

When they reached the floor beneath that occupied by the painter's studio, the old lady gently observed, 'Adelaide, you left the door open.'

'That was to come to my assistance,' said the painter, with a grateful smile.

'You came down just now, mother,' replied the young girl, with a blush.

'Would you like us to accompany you all the way downstairs?' asked the mother. 'The stairs are dark.'

'No, thank you, indeed, madame; I am much better.'

'Hold tightly by the rail.'

The two women remained on the landing to light the young

man, listening to the sound of his steps.

In order to set forth clearly all the exciting and unexpected interest this scene might have for the young painter, it must be told that he had only a few days since established his studio in the attics of this house, situated in the darkest and, therefore, the most muddy part of the Rue de Suresnes, almost opposite the Church of the Madeleine, and quite close to his rooms in the Rue des Champs-Elysees. The fame his talent had won him having made him one of the artists most dear to his country, he was beginning to feel free from want, and to use his own expression, was enjoying his last privations. Instead of going to his work in one of the studios near the city gates, where the moderate rents had hitherto been in proportion to his humble earnings, he had gratified a wish that was new every morning, by sparing himself a long walk, and the loss of much time, now more valuable than ever.

No man in the world would have inspired feelings of greater interest than Hippolyte Schinner if he would ever have consented to make acquaintance; but he did not lightly entrust to others the secrets of his life. He was the idol of a necessitous mother, who had brought him up at the cost of the severest privations. Mademoiselle Schinner, the daughter of an Alsatian farmer, had never been married. Her tender soul had been cruelly crushed, long ago, by a rich man, who did not pride himself on any great delicacy in his love affairs. The day when, as a young girl, in all the radiance of her beauty and all the triumph of her life, she suffered, at the cost of her heart and her sweet illusions, the disenchantment which falls on us so slowly and yet so quickly—for we try to postpone as long as possible our belief in evil, and it seems to come too soon—that day was a whole age of reflection, and it was also a day of religious thought and resignation. She refused the alms of the man who had betrayed her, renounced the world, and made a glory of her shame. She gave herself up entirely to her motherly love, seeking in it all her joys in exchange for the social pleasures to which she bid farewell. She lived by work, saving up a treasure for her son. And, in after years, a day, an hour repaid her amply for the long and weary sacrifices of her indigence.

At the last exhibition her son had received the Cross of the Legion of Honour. The newspapers, unanimous in hailing an unknown genius, still rang with sincere praises. Artists themselves acknowledged Schinner as a master, and dealers covered his canvases with gold pieces. At five-and-twenty Hippolyte Schinner, to whom his mother had transmitted her woman's soul, understood more clearly than ever his position in the world. Anxious to restore to his mother the pleasures of which society had so long robbed her, he lived for her, hoping by the aid of fame and fortune to see her one day happy, rich, respected, and surrounded by men of mark. Schinner had therefore chosen his friends among the most honourable and distinguished men. Fastidious in the selection of his intimates, he desired to raise still further a position which his talent had placed high. The work to which he had devoted himself from boyhood, by compelling him to dwell in solitude—the mother of great thoughts—had left him the beautiful beliefs which grace the early days of life. His adolescent soul was not closed to any of the thousand bashful emotions by which a young man is a being apart, whose heart abounds in joys, in poetry, in virginal hopes, puerile in the eyes of men of the world, but deep because they are single-hearted.

He was endowed with the gentle and polite manners which speak to the soul, and fascinate even those who do not understand them. He was well made. His voice, coming from his heart, stirred that of others to noble sentiments, and bore witness to his true modesty by a certain ingenuousness of tone. Those who saw him felt drawn to him by that attraction of the moral nature which men of science are happily unable to analyze; they would detect in it some phenomenon of galvanism, or the current of I know not what fluid, and express our sentiments in a formula of ratios of oxygen and electricity.

These details will perhaps explain to strong-minded persons and to men of fashion why, in the absence of the porter whom he had sent to the end of the Rue de la Madeleine to call him a coach, Hippolyte Schinner did not ask the man's wife any questions concerning the two women whose kindness of heart had shown itself in his behalf. But though he replied Yes or No to the inquiries, natural under the circumstances, which the good woman made as to his accident, and the friendly intervention of the tenants occupying the fourth floor, he could not hinder her from following the instinct of her kind; she mentioned the two strangers, speaking of them as prompted by the interests of her policy and the subterranean opinions of the porter's lodge.

'Ah,' said she, 'they were, no doubt, Mademoiselle Leseigneur and her mother, who have lived here these four years. We do not know exactly what these ladies do; in the morning, only till the hour of noon, an old woman who is half deaf, and who never speaks any more than a wall, comes in to help them; in the evening, two or three old gentlemen, with loops of ribbon, like you, monsieur, come to see them, and often stay very late. One of them comes in a carriage with servants, and is said to have sixty thousand francs a year. However, they are very quiet tenants, as you are, monsieur; and economical! they live on nothing, and as soon as a letter is brought they pay for it. It is a queer thing, monsieur, the mother's name is not the same as the daughter's. Ah, but when they go for a walk in the Tuileries, mademoiselle is very smart, and she never goes out but she is followed by a lot of young men; but she shuts the door in their face, and she is quite right. The proprietor would never allow—'

The coach having come, Hippolyte heard no more, and went home. His mother, to whom he related his adventure, dressed his wound afresh, and would not allow him to go to the studio next day. After taking advice, various treatments were prescribed, and Hippolyte remained at home three days. During this retirement his idle fancy recalled vividly, bit by bit, the details of the scene that had ensued on his fainting fit. The young girl's profile was clearly projected against the darkness of his inward vision; he saw once more the mother's faded features, or he felt the touch of Adelaide's hands. He remembered some gesture which at first had not greatly struck him, but whose exquisite grace was thrown into relief by memory; then an attitude, or the tones of a melodious voice, enhanced by the distance of remembrance, suddenly rose before him, as objects plunging to the bottom of deep waters come back to the surface.

So, on the day when he could resume work, he went early to his studio; but the visit he undoubtedly had a right to pay to his neighbours was the true cause of his haste; he had already forgotten the pictures he had begun. At the moment when a passion throws off its swaddling clothes, inexplicable pleasures are felt, known to those who have loved. So some readers will understand why the painter mounted the stairs to the fourth floor but slowly, and will be in the secret of the throbs that followed each other so rapidly in his heart at the moment when he saw the humble brown door of the rooms inhabited by Mademoiselle Leseigneur. This girl, whose name was not the same as her mother's, had aroused the young painter's deepest sympathies; he chose to fancy some similarity between himself and her as to their position, and attributed to her misfortunes of birth akin to his own. All the time he worked Hippolyte gave himself very willingly to thoughts of love, and made a great deal of noise to compel the two ladies to think of him, as he was thinking of them. He stayed late at the studio and dined there; then, at about seven o'clock, he went down to call on his neighbours.

No painter of manners has ventured to initiate us—perhaps out of modesty—into the really curious privacy of certain Parisian existences, into the secret of the dwellings whence emerge such fresh and elegant toilets, such brilliant women, who rich on the surface, allow the signs of very doubtful comfort to peep out in every part of their home. If, here, the picture is too boldly drawn, if you find it tedious in places, do not blame the description, which is, indeed, part and parcel of my story; for the appearance of the rooms inhabited by his two neighbours had a great influence on the feelings and hopes of Hippolyte Schinner.

The house belonged to one of those proprietors in whom there is a foregone and profound horror of repairs and decoration, one of the men who regard their position as Paris house-owners as a business. In the vast chain of moral species, these people hold a middle place between the miser and the usurer. Optimists in their own interests, they are all faithful to the Austrian status quo. If you speak of moving a cupboard or a door, of opening the most indispensable air-hole, their eyes flash, their bile rises, they rear like a frightened horse. When the wind blows down a few chimney-pots they are quite ill, and deprive themselves of an evening at the Gymnase or the Porte-Saint-Martin Theatre, 'on account of repairs'. Hippolyte, who had seen the performance gratis of a comical scene with Monsieur Molineux as concerning certain decorative repairs in his studio, was not surprised to see the dark greasy paint, the oily stains, spots, and other disagreeable accessories that varied the woodwork. And these stigmata of poverty are not altogether devoid of poetry in an artist's eyes.

Mademoiselle Leseigneur herself opened the door. On recognizing the young artist she bowed, and at the same time, with Parisian adroitness, and with the presence of mind that pride can lend, she turned round to shut the door in a glass partition through which Hippolyte might have caught sight of some linen hung by lines over patent ironing stoves, an old camp-bed, some wood-embers, charcoal, irons, a filter, the household crockery, and all the utensils familiar to a small household. Muslin curtains, fairly white, carefully screened this lumber-room—a 'capharnaum', as the French call such a domestic laboratory,—which was lighted by windows looking out on a neighbouring yard.

Hippolyte, with the quick eye of an artist, saw the uses, the furniture, the general effect and condition of this first room, thus cut in half. The more honourable half, which served both as ante-room and dining-room, was hung with an old salmon-rose-coloured paper, with a flock border, the manufacture of Reveillon, no doubt; the holes and spots had been carefully touched over with wafers. Prints representing the battles of Alexander, by Lebrun, in frames with the gilding rubbed off were symmetrically arranged on the walls. In the middle stood a massive mahogany table, old-fashioned in shape, and worn at the edges. A small stove, whose thin straight pipe was scarcely visible, stood in front of the chimney-place, but the hearth was occupied by a cupboard. By a strange contrast the chairs showed some remains of former splendour; they were of carved mahogany, but the red morocco seats, the gilt nails and reeded backs, showed as many scars as an old sergeant of the Imperial Guard.

This room did duty as a museum of certain objects, such as are never seen but in this kind of amphibious household; nameless objects with the stamp at once of luxury and penury. Among other curiosities Hippolyte noticed a splendidly finished telescope, hanging over the small discoloured glass that decorated the chimney. To harmonize with this strange collection of furniture, there was, between the chimney and the partition, a wretched sideboard of painted wood, pretending to be mahogany, of all woods the most impossible to imitate. But the slippery red quarries, the shabby little rugs in front of the chairs, and all the furniture, shone with the hard rubbing cleanliness which lends a treacherous lustre to old things by making their defects, their age, and their long service still more conspicuous. An indescribable odour pervaded the room, a mingled smell of the exhalations from the lumber room, and the vapours of the dining-room, with those from the stairs, though the window was partly open. The air from the street fluttered the dusty curtains, which were carefully drawn so as to hide the window bay, where former tenants had testified to their presence by various ornamental additions—a sort of domestic fresco.

Adelaide hastened to open the door of the inner room, where she announced the painter with evident pleasure. Hippolyte, who, of yore, had seen the same signs of poverty in his mother's home, noted them with the singular vividness of impression which characterizes the earliest acquisitions of memory, and entered into the details of this existence better than any one else would have done. As he recognized the facts of his life as a child, the kind young fellow felt neither scorn for disguised misfortune nor pride in the luxury he had lately conquered for his mother.

'Well, monsieur, I hope you no longer feel the effects of your fall,' said the old lady, rising from an antique armchair that stood by the chimney, and offering him a seat.

'No, madame. I have come to thank you for the kind care you gave me, and above all mademoiselle, who heard me fall.'

As he uttered this speech, stamped with the exquisite stupidity given to the mind by the first disturbing symptoms of true love, Hippolyte looked at the young girl. Adelaide was lighting the Argand lamp, no doubt that she might get rid of a tallow candle fixed in a large copper flat candlestick, and graced with a heavy fluting of grease from its guttering. She answered with a slight bow, carried the flat candlestick into the ante-room, came back, and after placing the lamp on the chimney shelf, seated herself by her mother, a little behind the painter, so as to be able to look at him at her ease, while apparently much interested in the burning of the lamp; the flame, checked by the damp in a dingy chimney, sputtered as it struggled with a charred and badly-trimmed wick. Hippolyte, seeing the large mirror that decorated the chimney-piece, immediately fixed his eyes on it to admire Adelaide. Thus the girl's little stratagem only served to embarrass them both.

While talking with Madame Leseigneur, for Hippolyte called her so, on the chance of being right, he examined the room, but unobtrusively and by stealth.

The Egyptian figures on the iron fire-dogs were scarcely visible, the hearth was so heaped with cinders; two brands tried to meet in front of a sham log of fire-brick, as carefully buried as a miser's treasure could ever be. An old Aubusson carpet, very much faded, very much mended, and as worn as a pensioner's coat, did not cover the whole of the tiled floor, and the cold struck to his feet. The walls were hung with a reddish paper, imitating figured silk with a yellow pattern. In the middle of the wall opposite the windows the painter saw a crack, and the outline marked on the paper of double-doors, shutting off a recess where Madame Leseigneur slept no doubt, a fact ill disguised by a sofa in front of the door. Facing the chimney, above a mahogany chest of drawers of handsome and tasteful design, was the portrait of an officer of rank, which the dim light did not allow him to see well; but from what he could make out he thought that the fearful daub must have been painted in China. The window-curtains of red silk were as much faded as the furniture, in red and yellow worsted work, as if this room 'contrived a double debt to pay'. On the marble top of the chest of drawers was a costly malachite tray, with a dozen coffee cups magnificently painted and made, no doubt, at Sevres. On the chimney shelf stood the omnipresent Empire clock: a warrior driving the four horses of a chariot, whose wheel bore the numbers of the hours on its spokes. The tapers in the tall candlesticks were yellow with smoke, and at each corner of the shelf stood a porcelain vase crowned with artificial flowers full of dust and stuck into moss.

In the middle of the room Hippolyte remarked a card-table ready for play, with new packs of cards. For an observer there was something heartrending in the sight of this misery painted up like an old woman who wants to falsify her face. At such a sight every man of sense must at once have stated to himself this obvious dilemma—either these two women are honesty itself, or they live by intrigue and gambling. But on looking at Adelaide, a man so pure-minded as Schinner could not but believe in her perfect innocence, and ascribe the incoherence of the furniture to honourable causes.

'My dear,' said the old lady to the young one, 'I am cold; make a little fire, and give me my shawl.'

Adelaide went into a room next the drawing-room, where she no doubt slept, and returned bringing her mother a cashmere shawl, which when new must have been very costly; the pattern was Indian; but it was old, faded and full of darns, and matched the furniture. Madame Leseigneur wrapped herself in it very artistically, and with the readiness of an old woman who wishes to make her words seem truth. The young girl ran lightly off to the lumber-room and reappeared with a bundle of small wood, which she gallantly threw on the fire to revive it.

It would be rather difficult to reproduce the conversation which followed among these three persons. Hippolyte, guided by the tact which is almost always the outcome of misfortune suffered in early youth, dared not allow himself to make the least remark as to his neighbours' situation, as he saw all about him the signs of ill-disguised poverty. The simplest question would have been an indiscretion, and could only be ventured on by old friendship. The painter was nevertheless absorbed in the thought of this concealed penury, it pained his generous soul; but knowing how offensive every kind of pity may be, even the friendliest, the disparity between his thoughts and his words made him feel uncomfortable.

The two ladies at first talked of painting, for women easily guess the secret embarrassment of a first call; they themselves feel it perhaps, and the nature of their mind supplies them with a thousand devices to put an end to it. By questioning the young man as to the material exercise of his art, and as to his studies, Adelaide and her mother emboldened him to talk. The indefinable nothings of their chat, animated by kind feeling, naturally led Hippolyte to flash forth remarks or reflections which showed the character of his habits and of his mind. Trouble had prematurely faded the old lady's face, formerly handsome, no doubt; nothing was left but the more prominent features, the outline, in a word, the skeleton of a countenance of which the whole effect indicated great shrewdness with much grace in the play of the eyes, in which could be discerned the expression peculiar to women of the old Court; an expression that cannot be defined in words. Those fine and mobile features might quite as well indicate bad feelings, and suggest astuteness and womanly artifice carried to a high pitch of wickedness, as reveal the refined delicacy of a beautiful soul.

Indeed, the face of a woman has this element of mystery to puzzle the ordinary observer, that the difference between frankness and duplicity, the genius for intrigue and the genius of the heart, is there inscrutable. A man gifted with the penetrating eye can read the intangible shade of difference produced by a more or less curved line, a more or less deep dimple, a more or less prominent feature. The appreciation of these indications lies entirely in the domain of intuition; this alone can lead to the discovery of what everyone is interested in concealing. The old lady's face was like the room she inhabited; it seemed as difficult to detect whether this squalor covered vice or the highest virtue, as to decide whether Adelaide's mother was an old coquette accustomed to weigh, to calculate, to sell everything, or a loving woman, full of noble feeling and amiable qualities. But at Schinner's age the first impulse of the heart is to believe in goodness. And indeed, as he studied Adelaide's noble and almost haughty brow, as he looked into her eyes full of soul and thought, he breathed, so to speak, the sweet and modest fragrance of virtue. In the course of the conversation he seized an opportunity of discussing portraits in general, to give himself a pretext for examining the frightful pastel, of which the colour had flown, and the chalk in many places fallen away.

'You are attached to that picture for the sake of the likeness, no doubt, mesdames, for the drawing is dreadful?' he said, looking at Adelaide.

'It was done at Calcutta, in great haste,' replied the mother in an agitated voice.

She gazed at the formless sketch with the deep absorption which memories of happiness produce when they are roused and fall on the heart like a beneficent dew to whose refreshing touch we love to yield ourselves up; but in the expression of the old lady's face there were traces too of perennial regret. At least, it was thus that the painter chose to interpret her attitude and countenance, and he presently sat down again by her side.

'Madame,' he said, 'in a very short time the colours of that pastel will have disappeared. The portrait will only survive in your memory. Where you will still see the face that is dear to you, others will see nothing at all. Will you allow me to reproduce the likeness on canvas? It will be more permanently recorded then than on that sheet of paper. Grant me, I beg, as a neighbourly favour, the pleasure of doing you this service. There are times when an artist is glad of a respite from his greater undertakings by doing work of less lofty pretensions, so it will be a recreation for me to paint that head.'

The old lady flushed as she heard the painter's words, and Adelaide shot one of those glances of deep feeling which seem to flash from the soul. Hippolyte wanted to feel some tie linking him with his two neighbours, to conquer a right to mingle in their life. His offer, appealing as it did to the liveliest affections of the heart, was the only one he could possibly make; it gratified his pride as an artist, and could not hurt the feelings of the ladies. Madame Leseigneur accepted, without eagerness or reluctance, but with the self-possession of a noble soul, fully aware of the character of bonds formed by such an obligation, while, at the same time, they are its highest glory as a proof of esteem.

'I fancy,' said the painter, 'that the uniform is that of a naval officer.'

'Yes,' she said, 'that of a captain in command of a vessel. Monsieur de Rouville—my husband—died at Batavia in consequence of a wound received in a fight with an English ship they fell in with off the Asiatic coast. He commanded a frigate of fifty-six guns and the *Revenge* carried ninety-six. The struggle was very unequal, but he defended his ship so bravely that he held out till nightfall and got away. When I came back to France Bonaparte was not yet in power, and I was refused a pension. When I applied again for it, quite lately, I was sternly informed that if the Baron de Rouville had emigrated I should not have lost him; that by this time he would have been a rear-admiral; finally, his Excellency quoted I know not what degree of forfeiture. I took this step, to which I was urged by my friends, only for the sake of my poor Adelaide. I have always hated the idea of holding out my hand as a beggar in the name of a grief which deprives a woman of voice and strength. I do not like this money valuation for blood irreparably spilt—'

'Dear mother, this subject always does you harm.'

In response to this remark from Adelaide, the Baronne Leseigneur bowed, and was silent.

'Monsieur,' said the young girl to Hippolyte, 'I had supposed that a painter's work was generally fairly quiet?'

At this question Schinner coloured, remembering the noise he had made. Adelaide said no more, and spared him a falsehood by rising at the sound of a carriage stopping at the door. She went into her own room, and returned carrying a pair of tall gilt candlesticks with partly burnt wax candles, which she quickly lighted, and without waiting for the bell to ring, she opened the door of the outer room, where she set the lamp down. The sound of a kiss given and received found an echo in Hippolyte's heart. The young man's impatience to see the man who treated Adelaide with so much familiarity was not immediately gratified; the newcomers had a conversation, which he thought very long, in an undertone, with the young girl.

At last Mademoiselle de Rouville returned, followed by two men, whose costume, countenance, and appearance are a long story.

The first, a man of about sixty, wore one of the coats invented, I believe, for Louis XVIII, then on the throne, in which the most difficult problem of the sartorial art had been solved by a tailor who ought to be immortal. That artist certainly understood the art of compromise, which was the moving genius of that period of shifting politics. Is it not a rare merit to be able to take the measure of the time? This coat, which the young men of the present day may conceive to be fabulous, was neither civil nor military, and might pass for civil or military by turns. Fleurs-de-lis were embroidered on the lapels of the back skirts. The gilt buttons also bore fleurs-de-lis; on the shoulders a pair of straps cried out for useless epaulettes; these military appendages were there like a petition without a recommendation. This old gentleman's coat was of dark blue cloth, and the buttonhole had blossomed into many coloured ribbons. He, no doubt, always carried his hat in his hand—a three cornered cocked hat, with a gold cord—for the snowy wings of his powdered hair showed not a trace of its pressure. He might have been taken for not more than fifty years of age, and seemed to enjoy robust health. While wearing the frank and loyal expression of the old emigres, his countenance also hinted at the easy habits of a libertine, at the light and reckless passions of the Musketeers formerly so famous in the annals of gallantry. His gestures, his attitude, and his manner proclaimed that he had no intention of correcting himself of his royalism, of his religion, or of his love affairs.

A really fantastic figure came in behind this specimen of 'Louis XIV's light infantry'—a nickname given by the Bonapartists to these venerable survivors of the Monarchy. To do it justice it ought to be made the principal object in the picture, and it is but an accessory. Imagine a lean, dry man, dressed like the former, but seeming to be only his reflection, or his shadow, if you will. The coat, new on the first, on the second was old; the powder in his hair looked less white, the gold of the fleurs-de-lis less bright, the shoulder straps more hopeless and dog's eared; his intellect seemed more feeble, his life nearer the fatal term than in the former. In short, he realized Rivarol's witticism on Champcenetz, 'He is the moonlight of me.' He was simply his double, a paler and poorer double, for there was between them all the difference that lies between the first and last impressions of a lithograph.

This speechless old man was a mystery to the painter, and always remained a mystery. The Chevalier, for he was a Chevalier, did not speak, nobody spoke to him. Was he a friend, a poor relation, a man who followed at the old gallant's heels as a lady companion does at an old lady's? Did he fill a place midway between a dog, a parrot, and a friend? Had he saved his patron's fortune, or only his life? Was he the Trim to another Captain Toby? Elsewhere, as at the Baronne de Rouville's, he always piqued curiosity without satisfying it. Who, after the Restoration, could remember the attachment which, before the Revolution, had bound this man to his friend's wife, dead now these twenty year?

The leader, who appeared the least dilapidated of these wrecks, came gallantly up to Madame de Rouville, kissed her hand, and sat down by her. The other bowed and placed himself not far from his model, at a distance represented by two chairs. Adelaide came behind the old gentleman's armchair and leaned her elbows on the back, unconsciously imitating the attitude given to Dido's sister by Guerin in his famous picture.

Though the gentleman's familiarity was that of a father, his freedom seemed at the moment to annoy the young girl.

'What, are you sulky with me?' he said.

Then he shot at Schinner one of those side-looks full of shrewdness and cunning, diplomatic looks, whose expression betrays the discreet uneasiness, the polite curiosity of well-bred people, and seems to ask, when they see a stranger, 'Is he one of us?'

'This is our neighbour,' said the old lady, pointing to Hippolyte. 'Monsieur is a celebrated painter, whose name must be known to you in spite of your indifference to the arts.'

The old man saw his friend's mischievous intent in suppressing the name, and bowed to the young man.

'Certainly,' said he. 'I heard a great deal about his pictures at the last Salon. Talent has immense privileges.' he added, observing the artist's red ribbon. 'That distinction, which we must earn at the cost of our blood and long service, you win in your youth; but all glory is of the same kindred,' he said, laying his hand on his Cross of Saint-Louis.

Hippolyte murmured a few words of acknowledgment, and was silent again, satisfied to admire with growing enthusiasm the beautiful girl's head that charmed him so much. He was soon lost in contemplation, completely forgetting the extreme misery of the dwelling. To him Adelaide's face stood out against a luminous atmosphere. He replied briefly to the questions addressed to him, which, by good luck, he heard, thanks to a singular faculty of the soul which sometimes seems to have a double consciousness. Who has not known what it is to sit lost in sad or delicious meditation, listening to its voice within, while attending to a conversation or to reading? An admirable duality which often helps us to tolerate a bore! Hope, prolific and smiling, poured out before him a thousand visions of happiness; and he refused to consider what was going on around him. As confiding as a child, it seemed to him base to analyze a pleasure.

After a short lapse of time he perceived that the old lady and her daughter were playing cards with the old gentleman. As to the satellite, faithful to his function as a shadow, he stood behind his friend's chair watching his game, and answering the player's mute inquiries by little approving nods, repeating the questioning gestures of the other countenance.

'Du Halga, I always lose,' said the gentleman.

'You discard badly,' replied the Baronne de Rouville.

'For three months now I have never won a single game,' said he.

'Have you the aces?' asked the old lady.

'Yes, one more to mark,' said he.

'Shall I come and advise you?' said Adelaide.

'No, no. Stay where I can see you. By Gad, it would be losing too much not to have you to look at!'

At last the game was over. The gentleman pulled out his purse, and, throwing two louis d'or on the table, not without temper—

'Forty francs,' he exclaimed, 'the exact sum.—Deuce take it! It is eleven o'clock.'

'It is eleven o'clock,' repeated the silent figure, looking at the painter.

The young man, hearing these words rather more distinctly than all the others, thought it time to retire. Coming back to the world of ordinary ideas, he found a few commonplace remarks to make, took leave of the Baroness, her daughter, and the two strangers, and went away, wholly possessed by the first raptures of true love, without attempting to analyze the little incidents of the evening.

On the morrow the young painter felt the most ardent desire to see Adelaide once more. If he had followed the call of his passion, he would have gone to his neighbour's door at six in the morning, when he went to his studio. However, he still was reasonable enough to wait till the afternoon. But as soon as he thought he could present himself to Madame de Rouville, he went downstairs, rang, blushing like a girl, shyly asked Mademoiselle Leseigneur, who came to let him in, to let him have the portrait of the Baron.

'But come in,' said Adelaide, who had no doubt heard him come down from the studio.

The painter followed, bashful and out of countenance, not knowing what to say, happiness had so dulled his wit. To see Adelaide, to hear the rustle of her skirt, after longing for a whole morning to be near her, after starting up a hundred time—'I will go down now'—and not to have gone; this was to him life so rich that such sensations, too greatly prolonged, would have worn out his spirit. The heart has the singular power of giving extraordinary value to mere nothings. What joy it is to a traveller to treasure a blade of grass, an unfamiliar leaf, if he has risked his life to pluck it! It is the same with the trifles of love.

The old lady was not in the drawing-room. When the young girl found herself there, alone with the painter, she brought a chair to stand on, to take down the picture; but perceiving that she could not unhook it without setting her foot on the chest of drawers, she turned to Hippolyte, and said with a blush:

'I am not tall enough. Will you get it down?'

A feeling of modesty, betrayed in the expression of her face and the tones of her voice, was the real motive of her request; and the young man, understanding this, gave her one of those glances of intelligence which are the sweetest language of love. Seeing that the painter had read her soul, Adelaide cast down her eyes with the instinct of reserve which is the secret of a maiden's heart. Hippolyte, finding nothing to say, and feeling almost timid, took down the picture, examined it gravely, carrying it to the light of the window, and then went away, without saying a word to Mademoiselle Leseigneur but, 'I will return it soon.'

During this brief moment they both went through one of those storms of agitation of which the effects in the soul may be compared to those of a stone flung into a deep lake. The most delightful waves of thought rise and follow each other, indescribable, repeated, and aimless, tossing the heart like the circular ripples, which for a long time fret the waters, starting from the point where the stone fell.

Hippolyte returned to the studio bearing the portrait. His easel was ready with a fresh canvas, and his palette set, his brushes cleaned, the spot and the light carefully chosen. And till the dinner hour he worked at the painting with the ardour artists throw into their whims. He went again that evening to the Baronne de Rouville's, and remained from nine till eleven. Excepting the different topics of conversation, this evening was exactly like the last. The two old men arrived at the same hour, the same game of piquet was played, the same speeches made by the players, the sum lost by Adelaide's friend was not less considerable than on the previous evening; only Hippolyte, a little bolder, ventured to chat with the young girl.

A week passed thus, and in the course of it the painter's feelings and Adelaide's underwent the slow and delightful transformations which bring two souls to a perfect understanding. Every day the look with which the girl welcomed her friend grew more intimate, more confiding, gayer, and more open; her voice and manner became more eager and more familiar. They laughed and talked together, telling each other their thoughts, speaking of themselves with the simplicity of two children who have made friends in a day, as much as if they had met constantly for three years. Schinner wished to be taught piquet. Being ignorant and a novice, he, of course, made blunder after blunder, and like the old man, he lost almost every game. Without having spoken a word of love the lovers knew that they were all in all to one another. Hippolyte enjoyed exerting his power over his gentle little friend, and many concessions were made to him by Adelaide, who, timid and devoted to him, was quite deceived by the assumed fits of temper, such as the least skilled lover and the most guileless girl can affect; and which they constantly play off, as spoilt children abuse the power they owe to their mother's affection. Thus all familiarity between the girl and the old Count was soon put a stop to. She understood the painter's melancholy, and the thoughts hidden in the furrows on his brow, from the abrupt tone of the few words he spoke when the old man unceremoniously kissed Adelaide's hands or throat.

Mademoiselle Leseigneur, on her part, soon expected her lover to give a short account of all his actions; she was so unhappy, so restless when Hippolyte did not come, she scolded him so effectually for his absence, that the painter had to give up seeing his other friends, and now went nowhere. Adelaide allowed the natural jealousy of women to be perceived when she heard that sometimes at eleven o'clock, on quitting the house, the painter still had visits to pay, and was to be seen in the most brilliant drawing-rooms of Paris. This mode of life, she assured him, was bad for his health; then, with the intense conviction to which the accent, the emphasis and the look of one we love lend so much weight, she asserted that a man who was obliged to expend his time and the charms of his wit on several women at once could not be the object of any very warm affection. Thus the painter was led, as much by the tyranny of his passion as by the exactions of a girl in love, to live exclusively in the little apartment where everything attracted him.

And never was there a purer or more ardent love. On both sides the same trustfulness, the same delicacy, gave their passion increase without the aid of those sacrifices by which many persons try to prove their affection. Between these two there was such a constant interchange of sweet emotion that they knew not which gave or received the most.

A spontaneous affinity made the union of their souls a close one. The progress of this true feeling was so rapid that two months after the accident to which the painter owed the happiness of knowing Adelaide, their lives were one life. From early morning the young girl, hearing footsteps overhead, could say to herself, 'He is there.' When Hippolyte went home to his mother at the dinner hour he never failed to look in on his neighbours, and in the evening he flew there at the accustomed hour with a lover's punctuality. Thus the most tyrannical woman or the most ambitious in the matter of love could not have found the smallest fault with the young painter. And Adelaide tasted of unmixed and unbounded happiness as she saw the fullest realization of the ideal of which, at her age, it is so natural to dream.

The old gentleman now came more rarely; Hippolyte, who had been jealous, had taken his place at the green table, and shared his constant ill-luck at cards. And sometimes, in the midst of his happiness, as he considered Madame de Rouville's disastrous position—for he had had more than one proof of her extreme poverty—an importunate thought would haunt him. Several times he had said to himself as he went home, 'Strange! Twenty francs every evening?' and he dared not confess to himself his odious suspicions.

He spent two months over the portrait, and when it was finished, varnished, and framed, he looked upon it as one of his best works. Madame la Baronne de Rouville had never spoken of it again. Was this from indifference or pride? The painter would not allow himself to account for this silence. He joyfully plotted with Adelaide to hang the picture in its place when Madame de Rouville should be out. So one day, during the walk her mother usually took in the Tuileries, Adelaide for the first time went up to Hippolyte's studio, on the pretext of seeing the portrait in the good light in which it had been painted. She stood speechless and motionless, but in ecstatic contemplation, in which all a woman's feelings were merged. For are they not all comprehended in boundless admiration for the man she loves? When the painter, uneasy at her silence, leaned forward to look at her, she held out her hand, unable to speak a word, but two tears fell from her eyes. Hippolyte took her hand and covered it with kisses; for a minute they looked at each other in silence, both longing to confess their love, and not daring. The painter kept her hand in his, and the same glow, the same throb, told them that their hearts were both beating wildly. The young girl, too greatly agitated, gently drew away from Hippolyte, and said, with a look of the utmost simplicity:

'You will make my mother very happy.'

'What, only your mother?' he asked.

'Oh, I am too happy.'

The painter bent his head and remained silent, frightened at the vehemence of the feelings which her tones stirred in his heart. Then, both understanding the perils of the situation, they went downstairs and hung up the picture in its place. Hippolyte dined for the first time with the Baroness, who, greatly overcome, and drowned in tears, must needs embrace him.

In the evening the old emigre, the Baron de Rouville's old comrade, paid the ladies a visit to announce that he had just been promoted to the rank of vice-admiral. His voyages by land over Germany and Russia had been counted as naval campaigns. On seeing the portrait he cordially shook the painter's hand, and exclaimed, 'By God! Though my old hulk does not deserve to be perpetuated, I would gladly give five hundred pistoles to see myself as like as that is to my dear old Rouville.'

At this hint the Baroness looked at her young friend and smiled, while her face lighted up with an expression of sudden gratitude. Hippolyte suspected that the old admiral wished to offer him the price of both portraits while paying for his own. His pride as an artist, no less than his jealousy perhaps, took offence at the thought, and he replied:

'Monsieur, if I were a portrait-painter I should not have done this one.'

The admiral bit his lip, and sat down to cards.

The painter remained near Adelaide, who proposed a dozen hands of piquet, to which he agreed. As he played he observed in Madame de Rouville an excitement over her game which surprised him. Never before had the old Baroness manifested so ardent a desire to win, or so keen a joy in fingering the old gentleman's gold pieces. During the evening evil suspicions troubled Hippolyte's happiness, and filled him with distrust. Could it be that Madame de Rouville lived by gambling? Was she playing at this moment to pay off some debt, or under the pressure of necessity? Perhaps she had not paid her rent. The old man seemed shrewd enough not to allow his money to be taken with impunity. What interest attracted him to this poverty-stricken house, he who was rich? Why, when he had formerly been so familiar with Adelaide, had he given up the rights he had acquired, and which were perhaps his due?

These involuntary reflections prompted him to watch the old man and the Baroness, whose meaning looks and certain sidelong glances cast at Adelaide displeased him. 'Am I being duped?' was Hippolyte's last idea—horrible, scathing, for he believed it just enough to be tortured by it. He determined to stay after the departure of the two old men, to confirm or dissipate his suspicions. He drew out his purse to pay Adelaide; but carried away by his poignant thoughts, he laid it on the table, falling into a reverie of brief duration; then, ashamed of his silence, he rose, answered some commonplace question from Madame de Rouville, and went close up to her to examine the withered features while he was talking to her.

He went away, racked by a thousand doubts. He had gone down but a few steps when he turned back to fetch the forgotten purse.

'I left my purse here!' he said to the young girl.

'No,' she said, reddening.

'I thought it was there,' and he pointed to the card-table. Not finding it, in his shame for Adelaide and the Baroness, he looked at them with a blank amazement that made them laugh, turned pale, felt his waistcoat, and said, 'I must have made a mistake. I have it somewhere no doubt.'

In one end of the purse there were fifteen louis d'or, and in the other some small change. The theft was so flagrant, and denied with such effrontery, that Hippolyte no longer felt a doubt as to his neighbours' morals. He stood still on the stairs, and got down with some difficulty; his knees shook, he felt dizzy, he was in a cold sweat, he shivered, and found himself unable to walk, struggling, as he was, with the agonizing shock caused by the destruction of all his hopes. And at this moment he found lurking in his memory a number of observations, trifling in themselves, but which corroborated his frightful suspicions, and which, by proving the certainty of this last incident, opened his eyes as to the character and life of these two women.

Had they really waited till the portrait was given them before robbing him of his purse? In such a combination the theft was even more odious. The painter recollected that for the last two or three evenings Adelaide, while seeming to examine with a girl's curiosity the particular stitch of the worn silk netting, was probably counting the coins in the purse, while making some light jests, quite innocent in appearance, but no doubt with the object of watching for a moment when the sum was worth stealing.

'The old admiral has perhaps good reasons for not marrying Adelaide, and so the Baroness has tried—'

But at this hypothesis he checked himself, not finishing his thought, which was contradicted by a very just reflection, 'If the Baroness hopes to get me to marry her daughter,' thought he, 'they would not have robbed me.'

Then, clinging to his illusions, to the love that already had taken such deep root, he tried to find a justification in some accident. 'The purse must have fallen on the floor,' said he to himself, 'or I left it lying on my chair. Or perhaps I have it about me—I am so absent-minded!' He searched himself with hurried movements, but did not find the ill-starred purse. His memory cruelly retraced the fatal truth, minute by minute. He distinctly saw the purse lying on the green cloth; but then, doubtful no longer, he excused Adelaide, telling himself that persons in misfortune should not be so hastily condemned. There was, of course, some secret behind this apparently degrading action. He would not admit that that proud and noble face was a lie.

At the same time the wretched rooms rose before him, denuded of the poetry of love which beautifies everything; he saw them dirty and faded, regarding them as emblematic of an inner life devoid of honour, idle and vicious. Are not our feelings written, as it were, on the things about us?

Next morning he rose, not having slept. The heartache, that terrible malady of the soul, had made rapid inroads. To lose the bliss we dreamed of, to renounce our whole future, is a keener pang than that caused by the loss of known happiness, however complete it may have been; for is not Hope better than Memory? The thoughts into which our spirit is suddenly plunged are like a shoreless sea, in which we may swim for a moment, but where our love is doomed to drown and die. And it is a frightful death. Are not our feelings the most glorious part of our life? It is this partial death which, in certain delicate or powerful natures, leads to the terrible ruin produced by disenchantment, by hopes and passions betrayed. Thus it was with the young painter. He went out at a very early hour to walk under the fresh shade of the Tuileries, absorbed in his thoughts, forgetting everything in the world.

There by chance he met one of his most intimate friends, a school-fellow and studio-mate, with whom he had lived on better terms than with a brother.

'Why, Hippolyte, what ails you?' asked Francois Souchet, the young sculptor who had just won the first prize, and was soon to set out for Italy.

'I am most unhappy,' replied Hippolyte gravely.

'Nothing but a love affair can cause you grief. Money, glory, respect—you lack nothing.'

Insensibly the painter was led into confidences, and confessed his love. The moment he mentioned the Rue de Suresnes, and a young girl living on the fourth floor, 'Stop, stop,' cried Souchet lightly. 'A little girl I see every morning at the Church of the Assumption, and with whom I have a flirtation. But, my dear fellow, we all know her. The mother is a Baroness. Do you really believe in a Baroness living up four flights of stairs? Brrr! Why, you are a relic of the golden age! We see the old mother here, in this avenue, every day; why, her face, her appearance, tell everything. What, have you not known her for what she is by the way she holds her bag?'

The two friends walked up and down for some time, and several young men who knew Souchet or Schinner joined them. The painter's adventure, which the sculptor regarded as unimportant, was repeated by him.

'So he, too, has seen that young lady!' said Souchet.

And then there were comments, laughter, innocent mockery, full of the liveliness familiar to artists, but which pained Hippolyte frightfully. A certain native reticence made him uncomfortable as he saw his heart's secret so carelessly handled, his passion rent, torn to tatters, a young and unknown girl, whose life seemed to be so modest, the victim of condemnation, right or wrong, but pronounced with such reckless indifference. He pretended to be moved by a spirit of contradiction, asking each for proofs of his assertions, and their jests began again.

'But, my dear boy, have you seen the Baroness' shawl?' asked Souchet.

'Have you ever followed the girl when she patters off to church in the morning?' said Joseph Bridau, a young dauber in Gros' studio.

'Oh, the mother has among other virtues a certain gray gown, which I regard as typical,' said Bixiou, the caricaturist.

'Listen, Hippolyte,' the sculptor went on. 'Come here at about four o'clock, and just study the walk of both mother and daughter. If after that you still have doubts! well, no one can ever make anything of you; you would be capable of marrying your porter's daughter.'

Torn by the most conflicting feelings, the painter parted from his friends. It seemed to him that Adelaide and her mother must be superior to these accusations, and at the bottom of his heart he was filled with remorse for having suspected the purity of this beautiful and simple girl. He went to his studio, passing the door of the rooms where Adelaide was, and conscious of a pain at his heart which no man can misapprehend. He loved Mademoiselle de Rouville so passionately that, in spite of the theft of the purse, he still worshipped her. His love was that of the Chevalier des Grieux admiring his mistress, and holding her as pure, even on the cart which carries such lost creatures to prison. 'Why should not my love keep her the purest of women? Why abandon her to evil and to vice without holding out a rescuing hand to her?'

The idea of this mission pleased him. Love makes a gain of everything. Nothing tempts a young man more than to play the part of a good genius to a woman. There is something inexplicably romantic in such an enterprise which appeals to a highly-strung soul. Is it not the utmost stretch of devotion under the loftiest and most engaging aspect? Is there not something grand in the thought that we love enough still to love on when the love of others dwindles and dies?

Hippolyte sat down in his studio, gazed at his picture without doing anything to it, seeing the figures through tears that swelled in his eyes, holding his brush in his hand, going up to the canvas as if to soften down an effect, but not touching it. Night fell, and he was still in this attitude. Roused from his moodiness by the darkness, he went downstairs, met the old admiral on the way, looked darkly at him as he bowed, and fled.

He had intended going in to see the ladies, but the sight of Adelaide's protector froze his heart and dispelled his purpose. For the hundredth time he wondered what interest could bring this old prodigal, with his eighty thousand francs a year, to this fourth story, where he lost about forty francs every evening; and he thought he could guess what it was.

The next and following days Hippolyte threw himself into his work, and to try to conquer his passion by the swift rush of ideas and the ardour of composition. He half succeeded. Study consoled him, though it could not smother the memories of so many tender hours spent with Adelaide.

One evening, as he left his studio, he saw the door of the ladies' rooms half open. Somebody was standing in the recess of the window, and the position of the door and the staircase made it impossible that the painter should pass without seeing Adelaide. He bowed coldly, with a glance of supreme indifference; but judging of the girl's suffering by his own, he felt an inward shudder as he reflected on the bitterness which that look and that coldness must produce in a loving heart. To crown the most delightful feast which ever brought joy to two pure souls, by eight days of disdain, of the deepest and most utter contempt!—A frightful conclusion. And perhaps the purse had been found, perhaps Adelaide had looked for her friend every evening.

This simple and natural idea filled the lover with fresh remorse; he asked himself whether the proofs of attachment given him by the young girl, the delightful talks, full of the love that had so charmed him, did not deserve at least an inquiry; were not worthy of some justification. Ashamed of having resisted the promptings of his heart for a whole week, and feeling himself almost a criminal in this mental struggle, he called the same evening on Madame de Rouville.

All his suspicions, all his evil thoughts vanished at the sight of the young girl, who had grown pale and thin.

'Good heavens! what is the matter?' he asked her, after greeting the Baroness.

Adelaide made no reply, but she gave him a look of deep melancholy, a sad, dejected look, which pained him.

'You have, no doubt, been working hard,' said the old lady. 'You are altered. We are the cause of your seclusion. That portrait had delayed some pictures essential to your reputation.'

Hippolyte was glad to find so good an excuse for his rudeness.

'Yes,' he said, 'I have been very busy, but I have been suffering—'

At these words Adelaide raised her head, looked at her lover, and her anxious eyes had now no hint of reproach.

'You must have thought us quite indifferent to any good or ill that may befall you?' said the old lady.

'I was wrong,' he replied. 'Still, there are forms of pain which we know not how to confide to any one, even to a friendship of older date than that with which you honour me.'

'The sincerity and strength of friendship are not to be measured by time. I have seen old friends who had not a tear to bestow on misfortune,' said the Baroness, nodding sadly.

'But you—what ails you?' the young man asked Adelaide.

'Oh, nothing,' replied the Baroness. 'Adelaide has sat up late for some nights to finish some little piece of woman's work, and would not listen to me when I told her that a day more or less did not matter—'

Hippolyte was not listening. As he looked at these two noble, calm faces, he blushed for his suspicions, and ascribed the loss of his purse to some unknown accident.

This was a delicious evening to him, and perhaps to her too.

There are some secrets which young souls understand so well. Adelaide could read Hippolyte's thoughts. Though he could not confess his misdeeds, the painter knew them, and he had come back to his mistress more in love, and more affectionate, trying thus to purchase her tacit forgiveness. Adelaide was enjoying such perfect, such sweet happiness, that she did not think she had paid too dear for it with all the grief that had so cruelly crushed her soul. And yet, this true concord of hearts, this understanding so full of magic charm, was disturbed by a little speech of Madame de Rouville's.

'Let us have our little game,' she said, 'for my old friend Kergarouet will not let me off.'

These words revived all the young painter's fears; he coloured as he looked at Adelaide's mother, but he saw nothing in her countenance but the expression of the frankest good nature; no double meaning marred its charm; its keenness was not perfidious, its humour seemed kindly, and no trace of remorse disturbed its equanimity.

He sat down to the card-table. Adelaide took side with the painter, saying that he did not know piquet, and needed a partner.

All through the game Madame de Rouville and her daughter exchanged looks of intelligence, which alarmed Hippolyte all the more because he was winning; but at last a final hand left the lovers in the old lady's debt.

To feel for some money in his pocket the painter took his hands off the table, and he then saw before him a purse which Adelaide had slipped in front of him without his noticing it; the poor child had the old one in her hand, and, to keep her countenance, was looking into it for the money to pay her mother. The blood rushed to Hippolyte's heart with such force that he was near fainting.

The new purse, substituted for his own, and which contained his fifteen gold louis, was worked with gilt beads. The rings and tassels bore witness to Adelaide's good taste, and she had no doubt spent all her little hoard in ornamenting this pretty piece of work. It was impossible to say with greater delicacy that the painter's gift could only be repaid by some proof of affection.

Hippolyte, overcome with happiness, turned to look at Adelaide and her mother, and saw that they were tremulous with pleasure and delight at their little trick. He felt himself mean, sordid, a fool; he longed to punish himself, to rend his heart. A few tears rose to his eyes; by an irresistible impulse he sprang up, clasped Adelaide in his arms, pressed her to his heart, and stole a kiss; then with the simple heartiness of an artist, 'I ask for her for my wife!' he exclaimed, looking at the Baroness.

Adelaide looked at him with half-wrathful eyes, and Madame de Rouville, somewhat astonished, was considering her reply, when the scene was interrupted by a ring at the bell. The old vice-admiral came in, followed by his shadow, and Madame Schinner. Having guessed the cause of the grief her son vainly endeavoured to conceal, Hippolyte's mother had made inquiries among her friends concerning Adelaide. Very justly alarmed by the calumnies which weighed on the young girl, unknown to the Comte de Kergarouet, whose name she learned from the porter's wife, she went to report them to the vice-admiral; and he, in his rage, declared 'he would crop all the scoundrels' ears for them.'

Then, prompted by his wrath, he went on to explain to Madame Schinner the secret of his losing intentionally at cards, because the Baronne's pride left him none but these ingenious means of assisting her.

When Madame Schinner had paid her respects to Madame de Rouville, the Baroness looked at the Comte de Kergarouet, at the Chevalier du Halga—the friend of the departed Comtesse de Kergarouet—at Hippolyte, and Adelaide, and said, with the grace that comes from the heart, 'So we are a family party this evening.'

8

A MAN OF BUSINESS

The word 'lorette' is a euphemism invented to describe the status of a personage, or a personage of a status, of which it is awkward to speak; the French Academie, in its modesty, having omitted to supply a definition out of regard for the age of its forty members. Whenever a new word comes to supply the place of an unwieldy circumlocution, its fortune is assured; the word 'lorette' has passed into the language of every class of society, even where the lorette herself will never gain an entrance. It was only invented in 1840, and derived beyond a doubt from the agglomeration of such swallows' nests about the Church of Our Lady of Loretto. This information is for etymoligists only. Those gentlemen would not be so often in a quandary if mediaeval writers had only taken such pains with details of contemporary manners as we take in these days of analysis and description.

Mlle. Turquet, or Malaga, for she is better known by her pseudonym (See *La fausse Maitresse*), was one of the earliest parishioners of that charming church. At the time to which this story belongs, that lighthearted and lively damsel gladdened the existence of a notary with a wife somewhat too bigoted, rigid, and frigid for domestic happiness.

Now, it so fell out that one Carnival evening Maitre Cardot was entertaining guests at Mlle. Turquet's house—Desroches the attorney, Bixiou of the caricatures, Lousteau the journalist, Nathan, and others; it is quite unnecessary to give any further description of these personages, all bearers of illustrious names in the *Comedie Humaine*. Young La Palferine, in spite of his title of Count and his great descent, which, alas! means a great descent in fortune likewise, had honoured the notary's little establishment with his presence.

At dinner, in such a house, one does not expect to meet the patriarchal beef, the skinny fowl and salad of domestic and family life, nor is there any attempt at the hypocritical conversation of drawing-rooms furnished with highly respectable matrons. When, alas! will respectability be charming? When will the women in good society vouchsafe to show rather less of their shoulders and rather more wit or geniality? Marguerite Turquet, the Aspasia of the Cirque-Olympique, is one of those frank, very living personalities to whom all is forgiven, such unconscious sinners are they, such intelligent penitents; of such as Malaga one might ask, like Cardot—a witty man enough, albeit a notary—to be well 'deceived'. And yet you must not think that any enormities were committed. Desroches and Cardot were good fellows grown too gray in the profession not to feel at ease with Bixiou, Lousteau, Nathan, and young La Palferine. And they on their side had too often had recourse to their legal advisers, and knew them too well to try to 'draw them out', in lorette language.

Conversation, perfumed with seven cigars, at first was as fantastic as a kid let loose, but finally it settled down upon the strategy of the constant war waged in Paris between creditors and debtors.

Now, if you will be so good as to recall the history and antecedents of the guests, you will know that in all Paris, you could scarcely find a group of men with more experience in this matter; the professional men on one hand, and the artists on the other, were something in the position of magistrates and criminals hobnobbing together. A set of Bixiou's drawings to illustrate life in the debtors' prison, led the conversation to take this particular turn; and from debtors' prisons they went to debts.

It was midnight. They had broken up into little knots round the table and before the fire, and gave themselves up to the burlesque fun which is only possible or comprehensible in Paris and in that particular region which is bounded by the Faubourg Montmartre, the Rue Chaussee d'Antin, the upper end of the Rue de Navarin and the line of the boulevards.

In ten minutes' time they had come to an end of all the deep reflections, all the moralizings, small and great, all the bad puns made on a subject already exhausted by Rabelais three hundred and fifty years ago. It was not a little to their credit that the pyrotechnic display was cut short with a final squib from Malaga.

'It all goes to the shoemakers,' she said. 'I left a milliner because she failed twice with my hats. The vixen has been here twenty-seven times to ask for twenty francs. She did not know that we never have twenty francs. One has a thousand francs, or one sends to one's notary for five hundred; but twenty francs I have never had in my life. My cook and my maid may, perhaps, have so much between them; but for my own part, I have nothing but credit, and I should lose that if I took to borrowing small sums. If I were to ask for twenty francs, I should have nothing to distinguish me from my colleagues that walk the boulevard.'

'Is the milliner paid?' asked La Palferine.

'Oh, come now, are you turning stupid?' said she, with a wink. 'She came this morning for the twenty-seventh time, that is how I came to mention it.'

'What did you do?' asked Desroches.

'I took pity upon her, and—ordered a little hat that I have just invented, a quite new shape. If Mlle. Amanda succeeds with it, she will say no more about the money, her fortune is made.'

'In my opinion,' put in Desroches, 'the finest things that I have seen in a duel of this kind give those who know Paris a far better picture of the city than all the fancy portraits that they paint. Some of you think that you know a thing or two,' he continued, glancing round at Nathan, Bixiou, La Palferine, and Lousteau, 'but the king of the ground is a certain Count, now busy ranging himself. In his time, he was supposed to be the cleverest, adroitest, canniest, boldest, stoutest, most subtle and experienced of all the pirates, who, equipped with fine manners, yellow kid gloves, and cabs, have ever sailed or ever will sail upon the stormy seas of Paris. He fears neither God nor man. He applies in private life the principles that guide the English Cabinet. Up to the time of his marriage, his life was one continual war, like—Lousteau's, for instance. I was, and am still his solicitor.'

'And the first letter of his name is Maxime de Trailles,' said La Palferine.

'For that matter, he has paid every one, and injured no one,' continued Desroches. 'But as your friend Bixiou was saying just now, it is a violation of the liberty of the subject to be made to pay in March when you have no mind to pay till October. By virtue of this article of his particular code, Maxime regarded a creditor's scheme for making him pay at once as a swindler's trick. It was a long time since he had grasped the significance of the bill of exchange in all its bearings, direct and remote. A young man once, in my place, called a bill of exchange the "asses' bridge" in his hearing. "No," said he, "it is the Bridge of Sighs; it is the shortest way to an execution." Indeed, his knowledge of commercial law was so complete, that a professional could not have taught him anything. At that time he had nothing, as you know. His carriage and horses were jobbed; he lived in his valet's house; and, by the way, he will be a hero to his valet to the end of the chapter, even after the marriage that he proposes to make. He belonged to three clubs, and dined at one of them whenever he did not dine out. As a rule, he was to be found very seldom at his own address—'

'He once said to me,' interrupted La Palferine, '"My one affection is the pretence that I make of living in the Rue Pigalle."'

'Well,' resumed Desroches, 'he was one of the combatants; and now for the other. You have heard more or less talk of one Claparon?'

'Had hair like this!' cried Bixiou, ruffling his locks till they stood on end. Gifted with the same talent for mimicking absurdities which Chopin the pianist possesses to so high a degree, he proceeded forthwith to represent the character with startling truth.

'He rolls his head like this when he speaks; he was once a commercial traveller; he has been all sorts of things—'

'Well, he was born to travel, for at this minute, as I speak, he is on the sea on his way to America,' said Desroches. 'It is his only chance, for in all probability he will be condemned by default as a fraudulent bankrupt next session.'

'Very much at sea!' exclaimed Malaga.

'For six or seven years this Claparon acted as man of straw, cat's paw, and scapegoat to two friends of ours, du Tillet and Nucingen; but in 1829 his part was so well known that—'

'Our friends dropped him,' put in Bixiou.

'They left him to his fate at last, and he wallowed in the mire,' continued Desroches. 'In 1833 he went into partnership with one Cerizet—'

'What! he that promoted a joint-stock company so nicely that the Sixth Chamber cut short his career with a couple of years in jail?' asked the lorette.

'The same. Under the Restoration, between 1823 and 1827, Cerizet's occupation consisted in first putting his name intrepidly to various paragraphs, on which the public prosecutor fastened with avidity, and subsequently marching off to prison. A man could make a name for himself with small expense in those days. The Liberal party called their provincial champion "the courageous Cerizet", and towards 1828 so much zeal received its reward in "general interest".'

'"General interest" is a kind of civic crown bestowed on the deserving by the daily press. Cerizet tried to discount the "general interest" taken in him. He came to Paris, and, with some help from capitalists in the Opposition, started as a broker, and conducted financial operations to some extent, the capital being found by a man in hiding, a skilful gambler who overreached himself, and in consequence, in July 1830, his capital foundered in the shipwreck of the Government.'

'Oh! it was he whom we used to call the System,' cried Bixiou.

'Say no harm of him, poor fellow,' protested Malaga. 'D'Estourny was a good sort.'

'You can imagine the part that a ruined man was sure to play in 1830 when his name in politics was "the courageous Cerizet". He was sent off into a very snug little sub-prefecture. Unluckily for him, it is one thing to be in opposition—any missile is good enough to throw, so long as the flight lasts; but quite another to be in office. Three months later, he was obliged to send in his resignation. Had he not taken it into his head to attempt to win popularity? Still, as he had done nothing as yet to imperil his title of "courageous Cerizet", the Government proposed by way of compensation that he should manage a newspaper; nominally an Opposition newspaper, but Ministerialist 'in petto'. So the fall of this noble nature was really due to the Government. To Cerizet, as manager of the paper, it was rather too evident that he was as a bird perched on a rotten bough; and then it was that he promoted that nice little joint-stock company, and thereby secured a couple of years in prison; he was caught, while more ingenious swindlers succeeded in catching the public.'

'We are acquainted with the more ingenious,' said Bixiou; 'let us say no ill of the poor fellow; he was nabbed; Couture allowed them to squeeze his cash-box; who would ever have thought it of him?'

'At all events, Cerizet was a low sort of fellow, a good deal damaged by low debauchery. Now for the duel I spoke about. Never did two tradesmen of the worst type, with the worst manners, the lowest pair of villains imaginable, go into partnership in a dirtier business. Their stock-in-trade consisted of the peculiar idiom of the man about town, the audacity of poverty, the cunning that comes of experience, and a special knowledge of Parisian capitalists, their origin, connections, acquaintances, and intrinsic value. This partnership of two "dabblers" (let the Stock Exchange term pass, for it is the only word which describes them), this partnership of dabblers did not last very long. They fought like famished curs over every bit of garbage.

'The earlier speculations of the firm of Cerizet and Claparon were, however, well planned. The two scamps joined forces with Barbet, Chaboisseau, Samanon, and usurers of that stamp, and bought up hopelessly bad debts.

'Claparon's place of business at that time was a cramped entresol in the Rue Chabannais—five rooms at a rent of seven hundred francs at most. Each partner slept in a little closet, so carefully closed from prudence, that my head-clerk could never get inside. The furniture of the other three rooms—an antechamber, a waiting-room, and a private office—would not have fetched three hundred francs altogether at a distress-warrant sale. You know enough of Paris to know the look of it; the stuffed horsehair-covered chairs, a table covered with a green cloth, a trumpery clock between a couple of candle sconces, growing tarnished under glass shades, the small gilt-framed mirror over the chimney-piece, and in the grate a charred stick or two of firewood which had lasted them for two winters, as my head-clerk put it. As for the office, you can guess what it was like—more letter-files than business letters, a set of common pigeon-holes for either partner, a cylinder desk, empty as the cash-box, in the middle of the room, and a couple of armchairs on either side of a coal fire.

The carpet on the floor was bought cheap at second-hand (like the bills and bad debts). In short, it was the mahogany furniture of furnished apartments which usually descends from one occupant of chambers to another during fifty years of service. Now you know the pair of antagonists.

'During the first three months of a partnership dissolved four months later in a bout of fisticuffs, Cerizet and Claparon bought up two thousand francs' worth of bills bearing Maxime's signature (since Maxime was his name), and filled a couple of letters to bursting with judgments, appeals, orders of the court, distress-warrants, application for stay of proceedings, and all the rest of it; to put it briefly, they had bills for three thousand two hundred francs odd centimes, for which they had given five hundred francs; the transfer being made under private seal, with special power of attorney, to save the expense of registration. Now it so happened at this juncture, Maxime, being of ripe age, was seized with one of the fancies peculiar to the man of fifty—'

'Antonia!' exclaimed La Palferine. 'That Antonia whose fortune I made by writing to ask for a toothbrush!'

'Her real name is Chocardelle,' said Malaga, not over well pleased by the fine-sounding pseudonym.

'The same,' continued Desroches.

'It was the only mistake Maxime ever made in his life. But what would you have, no vice is absolutely perfect?' put in Bixiou.

'Maxime had still to learn what sort of a life a man may be led into by a girl of eighteen when she is minded to take a header from her honest garret into a sumptuous carriage; it is a lesson that all statesmen should take to heart. At this time, de Marsay had just been employing his friend, our friend de Trailles, in the high comedy of politics. Maxime had looked high for his conquests; he had no experience of untitled women; and at fifty years he felt that he had a right to take a bite of the so-called wild fruit, much as a sportsman will halt under a peasant's apple-tree. So the Count found a reading-room for Mlle. Chocardelle, a rather smart little place to be had cheap, as usual—'

'Pooh!' said Nathan. 'She did not stay in it six months. She was too handsome to keep a reading-room.'

'Perhaps you are the father of her child?' suggested the lorette. Desroches resumed.

'Since the firm bought up Maxime's debts, Cerizet's likeness to a bailiff's officer grew more and more striking, and one morning after seven fruitless attempts he succeeded in penetrating into the Count's presence. Suzon, the old man-servant, albeit he was by no means in his novitiate, at last mistook the visitor for a petitioner, come to propose a thousand crowns if Maxime would obtain a license to sell postage stamps for a young lady. Suzon, without the slightest suspicion of the little scamp, a thoroughbred Paris street-boy into whom prudence had been rubbed by repeated personal experience of the police-courts, induced his master to receive him. Can you see the man of business, with an uneasy eye, a bald forehead, and scarcely any hair on his head, standing in his threadbare jacket and muddy boots—'

'What a picture of a Dun!' cried Lousteau.

'—standing before the Count, that image of flaunting Debt, in his blue flannel dressing-gown, slippers worked by some Marquise or other, trousers of white woollen stuff, and a dazzling shirt? There he stood, with a gorgeous cap on his black dyed hair, playing with the tassels at his waist—'

"Tis a bit of genre for anybody who knows what the pretty little morning room, hung with silk and full of valuable paintings, where Maxime breakfasts,' said Nathan. 'You tread on a Smyrna carpet, you admire the sideboards filled with curiosities and rarities fit to make a King of Saxony envious—'

'Now for the scene itself,' said Desroches, and the deepest silence followed.

'"Monsieur le Comte," began Cerizet, "I have come from a M.

Charles Claparon, who used to be a banker—"

"'Ah! poor devil, and what does he want with me?'"

"'Well, he is at present your creditor for a matter of three thousand two hundred francs, seventy-five centimes, principal, interest, and costs—'"

"'Coutelier's business?' put in Maxime, who knew his affairs as a pilot knows his coast.

"'Yes, Monsieur le Comte,' said Cerizet with a bow. 'I have come to ask your intentions.'

"'I shall only pay when the fancy takes me,' returned Maxime, and he rang for Suzon. 'It was very rash of Claparon to buy up bills of mine without speaking to me beforehand. I am sorry for him, for he did so very well for such a long time as a man of straw for friends of mine. I always said that a man must really be weak in his intellect to work for men that stuff themselves with millions, and to serve them so faithfully for such low wages. And now here he gives me another proof of his stupidity! Yes, men deserve what they get. It is your own doing whether you get a crown on your forehead or a bullet through your head; whether you are a millionaire or a porter, justice is always done you. I cannot help it, my dear fellow; I myself am not a king, I stick to my principles. I have no pity for those that put me to expense or do not know their business as creditors.—Suzon! my tea! Do you see this gentleman?' he continued when the man came in. 'Well, you have allowed yourself to be taken in, poor old boy. This gentleman is a creditor; you ought to have known him by his boots. No friend nor foe of mine, nor those that are neither and want something of me, come to see me on foot.—My dear M. Cerizet, do you understand? You will not wipe your boots on my carpet again" (looking as he spoke at the mud that whitened the enemy's soles). "Convey my compliments and sympathy to Claparon, poor buffer, for I shall file this business under the letter Z.'

'All this with an easy good-humour fit to give a virtuous

citizen the colic.

'"You are wrong, Monsieur le Comte," retorted Cerizet, in a slightly peremptory tone. "We will be paid in full, and that in a way which you may not like. That is why I came to you first in a friendly spirit, as is right and fit between gentlemen—"

'"Oh! so that is how you understand it?" began Maxime, enraged by this last piece of presumption. There was something of Talleyrand's wit in the insolent retort, if you have quite grasped the contrast between the two men and their costumes. Maxime scowled and looked full at the intruder; Cerizet not merely endured the glare of cold fury, but even returned it, with an icy, cat-like malignance and fixity of gaze.

'"Very good, sir, go out—"

'"Very well, good-day, Monsieur le Comte. We shall be quits before six months are out."

'"If you can steal the amount of your bill, which is legally due I own, I shall be indebted to you, sir," replied Maxime. "You will have taught me a new precaution to take. I am very much your servant."

'"Monsieur le Comte," said Cerizet, "it is I, on the contrary, who am yours."

'Here was an explicit, forcible, confident declaration on either side. A couple of tigers confabulating, with the prey before them, and a fight impending, would have been no finer and no shrewder than this pair; the insolent fine gentleman as great a blackguard as the other in his soiled and mud-stained clothes.

'Which will you lay your money on?' asked Desroches, looking round at an audience, surprised to find how deeply it was interested.

'A pretty story!' cried Malaga. 'My dear boy, go on, I beg of you. This goes to one's heart.'

'Nothing commonplace could happen between two fighting-cocks of that calibre,' added La Palferine.

'Pooh!' cried Malaga. 'I will wager my cabinet-maker's invoice (the fellow is dunning me) that the little toad was too many for Maxime.'

'I bet on Maxime,' said Cardot. 'Nobody ever caught him napping.'

Desroches drank off a glass that Malaga handed to him.

'Mlle. Chocardelle's reading-room,' he continued, after a pause, 'was in the Rue Coquenard, just a step or two from the Rue Pigalle where Maxime was living. The said Mlle. Chocardelle lived at the back on the garden side of the house, beyond a big dark place where the books were kept. Antonia left her aunt to look after the business—'

'Had she an aunt even then?' exclaimed Malaga. 'Hang it all, Maxime did things handsomely.'

'Alas! it was a real aunt,' said Desroches; 'her name was—let me see—'

'Ida Bonamy,' said Bixiou.

'So as Antonia's aunt took a good deal of the work off her hands, she went to bed late and lay late of a morning, never showing her face at the desk until the afternoon, some time between two and four. From the very first her appearance was enough to draw custom. Several elderly men in the quarter used to come, among them a retired coach-builder, one Croizeau. Beholding this miracle of female loveliness through the window-panes, he took it into his head to read the newspapers in the beauty's reading-room; and a sometime custom-house officer, named Denisart, with a ribbon in his button-hole, followed the example. Croizeau chose to look upon Denisart as a rival. "Monsieur," he said afterwards, "I did not know what to buy for you!"

'That speech should give you an idea of the man. The Sieur Croizeau happens to belong to a particular class of old man which should be known as "Coquerels" since Henri Monnier's time; so well did Monnier render the piping voice, the little mannerisms, little queue, little sprinkling of powder, little movements of the head, prim little manner, and tripping gait in the part of Coquerel in *La Famille Improvisee*. This Croizeau used to hand over his halfpence with a flourish and a "There, fair lady!"

'Mme. Ida Bonamy the aunt was not long in finding out through a servant that Croizeau, by popular report of the neighbourhood of the Rue de Buffault, where he lived, was a man of exceeding stinginess, possessed of forty thousand francs per annum. A week after the instalment of the charming librarian he was delivered of a pun:

'"You lend me books (livres), but I give you plenty of francs in return," said he.

'A few days later he put on a knowing little air, as much as to say, "I know you are engaged, but my turn will come one day; I am a widower."

'He always came arrayed in fine linen, a cornflower blue coat, a paduasoy waistcoat, black trousers, and black ribbon bows on the double soled shoes that creaked like an abbe's; he always held a fourteen franc silk hat in his hand.

'"I am old and I have no children," he took occasion to confide to the young lady some few days after Cerizet's visit to Maxime. "I hold my relations in horror. They are peasants born to work in the fields. Just imagine it, I came up from the country with six francs in my pocket, and made my fortune here. I am not proud. A pretty woman is my equal. Now would it not be nicer to be Mme. Croizeau for some years to come than to do a Count's pleasure for a twelvemonth? He will go off and leave you some time or other; and when that day comes, you will think of me...your servant, my pretty lady!"

'All this was simmering below the surface. The slightest approach at love-making was made quite on the sly. Not a soul suspected that the trim little old fogy was smitten with Antonia; and so prudent was the elderly lover, that no rival could have guessed anything from his behaviour in the reading-room. For a couple of months Croizeau watched the retired custom-house official; but before the third month was out he had good reason to believe that his suspicions were groundless. He exerted his ingenuity to scrape an acquaintance with Denisart, came up with him in the street, and at length seized his opportunity to remark, "It is a fine day, sir!"

'Whereupon the retired official responded with, "Austerlitz weather, sir. I was there myself—I was wounded indeed, I won my Cross on that glorious day."

'And so from one thing to another the two drifted wrecks of the Empire struck up an acquaintance. Little Croizeau was attached to the Empire through his connection with Napoleon's sisters. He had been their coach-builder, and had frequently dunned them for money; so he gave out that he "had had relations with the Imperial family". Maxime, duly informed by Antonia of the "nice old man's" proposals (for so the aunt called Croizeau), wished to see him. Cerizet's declaration of war had so far taken effect that he of the yellow kid gloves was studying the position of every piece, however insignificant, upon the board; and it so happened that at the mention of that "nice old man", an ominous tinkling sounded in his ears. One evening, therefore, Maxime seated himself among the book-shelves in the dimly lighted back room, reconnoitred the seven or eight customers through the chink between the green curtains, and took the little coach-builder's measure. He gauged the man's infatuation, and was very well satisfied to find that the varnished doors of a tolerably sumptuous future were ready to turn at a word from Antonia so soon as his own fancy had passed off.

'"And that other one yonder?" asked he, pointing out the stout fine-looking elderly man with the Cross of the Legion of Honour. "Who is he?"

'"A retired custom-house officer."

"'The cut of his countenance is not reassuring," said Maxime, beholding the Sieur Denisart.

'And indeed the old soldier held himself upright as a steeple. His head was remarkable for the amount of powder and pomatum bestowed upon it; he looked almost like a postilion at a fancy ball. Underneath that felted covering, moulded to the top of the wearer's cranium, appeared an elderly profile, half-official, half-soldierly, with a comical admixture of arrogance,—altogether something like caricatures of the *Constitutionnel*. The sometime official finding that age, and hair-powder, and the conformation of his spine made it impossible to read a word without spectacles, sat displaying a very creditable expanse of chest with all the pride of an old man with a mistress. Like old General Montcornet, that pillar of the Vaudeville, he wore earrings. Denisart was partial to blue; his roomy trousers and well-worn greatcoat were both of blue cloth.

"'How long is it since that old fogy came here?" inquired Maxime, thinking that he saw danger in the spectacles.

"'Oh, from the beginning," returned Antonia, "pretty nearly two months ago now."

"'Good," said Maxime to himself, "Cerizet only came to me a month ago.—Just get him to talk," he added in Antonia's ear; "I want to hear his voice."

"'Pshaw," said she, "that is not so easy. He never says a word to me."

"'Then why does he come here?" demanded Maxime.

"'For a queer reason," returned the fair Antonia. 'In the first place, although he is sixty-nine, he has a fancy; and because he is sixty-nine, he is as methodical as a clock face. Every day at five o'clock the old gentleman goes to dine with her in the Rue de la Victoire. (I am sorry for her.) Then at six o'clock, he comes here, reads steadily at the papers for four hours, and goes back at ten o'clock. Daddy Croizeau says that he knows M. Denisart's motives, and approves his conduct; and in his place, he would do the same. So I know exactly what to expect. If ever I am Mme. Croizeau, I shall have four hours to myself between six and ten o'clock."

'Maxime looked through the directory, and found the following reassuring item:

'"DENISART, retired custom-house officer, Rue de la Victoire."

'His uneasiness vanished.

'Gradually the Sieur Denisart and the Sieur Croizeau began to exchange confidences. Nothing so binds two men together as a similarity of views in the matter of womankind. Daddy Croizeau went to dine with "M. Denisart's fair lady", as he called her. And here I must make a somewhat important observation.

'The reading-room had been paid for half in cash, half in bills signed by the said Mlle. Chocardelle. The *quart d'heure de Rabelais* arrived; the Count had no money. So the first bill of three thousand francs was met by the amiable coach-builder; that old scoundrel Denisart having recommended him to secure himself with a mortgage on the reading-room.

'"For my own part," said Denisart, "I have seen pretty doings from pretty women. So in all cases, even when I have lost my head, I am always on my guard with a woman. There is this creature, for instance; I am madly in love with her; but this is not her furniture; no, it belongs to me. The lease is taken out in my name."

'You know Maxime! He thought the coach-builder uncommonly green. Croizeau might pay all three bills, and get nothing for a long while; for Maxime felt more infatuated with Antonia than ever.'

'I can well believe it,' said La Palferine. 'She is the bella Imperia of our day.'

'With her rough skin!' exclaimed Malaga; 'So rough, that she ruins herself in bran baths!'

'Croizeau spoke with a coach-builder's admiration of the sumptuous furniture provided by the amorous Denisart as a setting for his fair one, describing it all in detail with diabolical complacency for Antonia's benefit,' continued Desroches. 'The ebony chests inlaid with mother-of-pearl and gold wire, the Brussels carpets, a mediaeval bedstead worth three thousand francs, a Boule clock, candelabra in the four corners of the dining-room, silk curtains, on which Chinese patience had wrought pictures of birds, and hangings over the doors, worth more than the portress that opened them.

"'And that is what *you* ought to have, my pretty lady.—And that is what I should like to offer you," he would conclude. "I am quite aware that you scarcely care a bit about me; but, at my age, we cannot expect too much. Judge how much I love you; I have lent you a thousand francs. I must confess that, in all my born days, I have not lent anybody that much—"

'He held out his penny as he spoke, with the important air of a man that gives a learned demonstration.

'That evening at the Varietes, Antonia spoke to the Count.

"'A reading-room is very dull, all the same," said she; "I feel that I have no sort of taste for that kind of life, and I see no future in it. It is only fit for a widow that wishes to keep body and soul together, or for some hideously ugly thing that fancies she can catch a husband with a little finery."

"'It was your own choice," returned the Count. Just at that moment, in came Nucingen, of whom Maxime, king of lions (the "yellow kid gloves" were the lions of that day) had won three thousand francs the evening before. Nucingen had come to pay his gaming debt.

"'Ein writ of attachment haf shoost peen served on me by der order of dot teufel Glabaron," he said, seeing Maxime's astonishment.

"'Oh, so that is how they are going to work, is it?" cried Maxime. "They are not up to much, that pair—"

"'It makes not," said the banker, "bay dem, for dey may apply demselfs to oders pesides, und do you harm. I dake dees bretty voman to vitness dot I haf baid you dees morning, long pefore dat writ vas serfed."'

'Queen of the boards,' smiled La Palferine, looking at Malaga, 'thou art about to lose thy bet.'

'Once, a long time ago, in a similar case,' resumed Desroches, 'a too honest debtor took fright at the idea of a solemn declaration in a court of law, and declined to pay Maxime after notice was given. That time we made it hot for the creditor by piling on writs of attachment, so as to absorb the whole amount in costs—'

'Oh, what is that?' cried Malaga; 'it all sounds like gibberish to me. As you thought the sturgeon so excellent at dinner, let me take out the value of the sauce in lessons in chicanery.'

'Very well,' said Desroches. 'Suppose that a man owes you money, and your creditors serve a writ of attachment upon him; there is nothing to prevent all your other creditors from doing the same thing. And now what does the court do when all the creditors make application for orders to pay? The court divides the whole sum attached, proportionately among them all. That division, made under the eye of a magistrate, is what we call a contribution. If you owe ten thousand francs, and your creditors issue writs of attachment on a debt due to you of a thousand francs, each one of them gets so much per cent, "so much in the pound", in legal phrase; so much (that means) in proportion to the amounts severally claimed by the creditors. But—the creditors cannot touch the money without a special order from the clerk of the court. Do you guess what all this work drawn up by a judge and prepared by attorneys must mean? It means a quantity of stamped paper full of diffuse lines and blanks, the figures almost lost in vast spaces of completely empty ruled columns. The first proceeding is to deduct the costs. Now, as the costs are precisely the same whether the amount attached is one thousand or one million francs, it is not difficult to eat up three thousand francs (for instance) in costs, especially if you can manage to raise counter applications.'

'And an attorney always manages to do it,' said Cardot. 'How many a time one of you has come to me with, "What is there to be got out of the case?"'

'It is particularly easy to manage it if the debtor eggs you on to run up costs till they eat up the amount. And, as a rule, the Count's creditors took nothing by that move, and were out of pocket in law and personal expenses. To get money out of so experienced a debtor as the Count, a creditor should really be in a position uncommonly difficult to reach; it is a question of being creditor and debtor both, for then you are legally entitled to work the confusion of rights, in law language—'

'To the confusion of the debtor?' asked Malaga, lending an attentive ear to this discourse.

'No, the confusion of rights of debtor and creditor, and pay yourself through your own hands. So Claparon's innocence in merely issuing writs of attachment eased the Count's mind. As he came back from the Varietes with Antonia, he was so much the more taken with the idea of selling the reading-room to pay off the last two thousand francs of the purchase-money, because he did not care to have his name made public as a partner in such a concern. So he adopted Antonia's plan. Antonia wished to reach the higher ranks of her calling, with splendid rooms, a maid, and a carriage; in short, she wanted to rival our charming hostess, for instance—'

'She was not woman enough for that,' cried the famous beauty of the Circus; 'still, she ruined young d'Esgrignon very neatly.'

'Ten days afterwards, little Croizeau, perched on his dignity, said almost exactly the same thing, for the fair Antonia's benefit,' continued Desroches.

'"Child," said he, "your reading-room is a hole of a place. You will lose your complexion; the gas will ruin your eyesight. You ought to come out of it; and, look here, let us take advantage of an opportunity. I have found a young lady for you that asks no better than to buy your reading-room. She is a ruined woman with nothing before her but a plunge into the river; but she had four thousand francs in cash, and the best thing to do is to turn them to account, so as to feed and educate a couple of children."

"'Very well. It is kind of you, Daddy Croizeau,' said Antonia.

"'Oh, I shall be much kinder before I have done. Just imagine it, poor M. Denisart has been worried into the jaundice! Yes, it has gone to the liver, as it usually does with susceptible old men. It is a pity he feels things so. I told him so myself; I said, 'Be passionate, there is no harm in that, but as for taking things to heart—draw the line at that! It is the way to kill yourself.'—Really, I would not have expected him to take on so about it; a man that has sense enough and experience enough to keep away as he does while he digests his dinner—"

"'But what is the matter?' inquired Mlle. Chocardelle.

"'That little baggage with whom I dined has cleared out and left him!... Yes. Gave him the slip without any warning but a letter, in which the spelling was all to seek."

"'There, Daddy Croizeau, you see what comes of boring a woman—'

"'It is indeed a lesson, my pretty lady,' said the guileful Croizeau. 'Meanwhile, I have never seen a man in such a state. Our friend Denisart cannot tell his left hand from his right; he will not go back to look at the 'scene of his happiness', as he calls it. He has so thoroughly lost his wits, that he proposes that I should buy all Hortense's furniture (Hortense was her name) for four thousand francs."

"'A pretty name,' said Antonia.

"'Yes. Napoleon's stepdaughter was called Hortense. I built carriages for her, as you know.'

"'Very well, I will see', said cunning Antonia; 'begin by sending this young woman to me.'

'Antonia hurried off to see the furniture, and came back

fascinated. She brought Maxime under the spell of antiquarian enthusiasm. That very evening the Count agreed to the sale of the reading-room. The establishment, you see, nominally belonged to Mlle. Chocardelle. Maxime burst out laughing at the idea of little Croizeau's finding him a buyer. The firm of Maxime and Chocardelle was losing two thousand francs, it is true, but what was the loss compared with four glorious thousand-franc notes in hand? "Four thousand francs of live coin!—there are moments in one's life when one would sign bills for eight thousand to get them," as the Count said to me.

'Two days later the Count must see the furniture himself, and took the four thousand francs upon him. The sale had been arranged; thanks to little Croizeau's diligence, he pushed matters on; he had "come round" the widow, as he expressed it. It was Maxime's intention to have all the furniture removed at once to a lodging in a new house in the Rue Tronchet, taken in the name of Mme. Ida Bonamy; he did not trouble himself much about the nice old man that was about to lose his thousand francs. But he had sent beforehand for several big furniture vans.

'Once again he was fascinated by the beautiful furniture which a wholesale dealer would have valued at six thousand francs. By the fireside sat the wretched owner, yellow with jaundice, his head tied up in a couple of printed handkerchiefs, and a cotton night-cap on top of them; he was huddled up in wrappings like a chandelier, exhausted, unable to speak, and altogether so knocked to pieces that the Count was obliged to transact his business with the man-servant. When he had paid down the four thousand francs, and the servant had taken the money to his master for a receipt, Maxime turned to tell the man to call up the vans to the door; but even as he spoke, a voice like a rattle sounded in his ears.

'"It is not worth while, Monsieur le Comte. You and I are quits; I have six hundred and thirty francs fifteen centimes to give you!"

'To his utter consternation, he saw Cerizet, emerged from

his wrappings like a butterfly from the chrysalis, holding out the accursed bundle of documents.

"'When I was down on my luck, I learned to act on the stage,' added Cerizet. 'I am as good as Bouffe at old men.'

"'I have fallen among thieves!' shouted Maxime.

"'No, Monsieur le Comte, you are in Mlle. Hortense's house. She is a friend of old Lord Dudley's; he keeps her hidden away here; but she has the bad taste to like your humble servant.'

"'If ever I longed to kill a man,' so the Count told me afterwards, 'it was at that moment; but what could one do? Hortense showed her pretty face, one had to laugh. To keep my dignity, I flung her the six hundred francs. "There's for the girl," said I.'"

'That is Maxime all over!' cried La Palferine.

'More especially as it was little Croizeau's money,' added Cardot the profound.

'Maxime scored a triumph,' continued Desroches, 'for Hortense exclaimed, "Oh, if I had only known that it was you!"'

'A pretty "confusion" indeed!' put in Malaga. 'You have lost, milord,' she added turning to the notary.

And in this way the cabinetmaker, to whom Malaga owed a hundred crowns, was paid.

ABOUT TERRY O'BRIEN

Terry O'Brien is an academic with three decades of experience in teaching language and communication skills in India and abroad. He also headed a college under the auspices of the University of Delhi.

A prolific writer, with several books to his credit, Terry O'Brien is a reputed professional motivational speaker and a quizmaster.